ESCAPE FROM GROUND ZERO

A NOVEL

by

MICHAEL ZOGLIO

Escape from Ground Zero

Copyright © 2025 by Michael Zoglio

This is a work of fiction. Names, characters, businesses, places, and incidents are products of the author's imagination or are used fictitiously. Any resemblance to actual persons, living or dead, events, or locales is coincidental.

DEDICATION

To Sue, for a lifetime of caring, encouragement, and support.

PREFACE

Like so many others, I was personally shocked and deeply saddened by the terrorist attacks of September 11, 2001. The enormity of the tragedy was overwhelming: the loss of life, the lasting impact on the families, friends, first responders, and all Americans.

I was also struck by the overwhelming chaos of that day. As a former private investigator with experience in locating missing persons, I knew how, in rare instances throughout history, individuals have used extreme situations to vanish and start anew. The idea that someone could have used the 9/11 chaos to disappear was a haunting thought that stayed with me for years.

Now, more than two decades later, time has allowed some emotional distance, and my haunting thought has grown into this fictional narrative. It is entirely born of my imagination and crafted with respect for the real events and the people affected by them. None of the characters in the book are real except for the named hijacker.

For authenticity of setting, I visited Ground Zero and the surrounding areas in Manhattan, read survivor accounts and first responder testimonies, and utilized resources such as historical diagrams and documentation. While I have taken care to represent New York City, New Orleans, and Key West accurately, some details are fictionalized in service of the story.

Most importantly, I want to express my sincere condolences to the families and friends of those who were lost on 9/11. This story is not meant to suggest any truth beyond the fictional world I've created. It is a tale of mystery and human complexity, set against the backdrop of one of the most defining moments in American history.

Michael Zoglio
Bonita Springs, Florida
April 2025

CHAPTER 1

THE MUSEUM JOB

Boston, March 17, 1990

ST. Patrick's Day evening. The streets were full of drunks and green.

The stolen red Dodge Daytona sat in shadow. Two men inside. Coffee steamed the windshield. They wore blue, with badges clipped to their coats. Not real ones.

One checked his watch. 1:24 a.m. They were late. Too many people still on the street.

"Ten more minutes," the driver said.

The other nodded. They waited in silence.

When the sidewalk emptied, they got out. They walked to the side door of the Isabella Stewart Gardner Museum. Buzzed security.

A voice came through the intercom. "What's going on?"

"Boston Police," one said. "Responding to a disturbance in the courtyard."

"Didn't hear anything," the security guard responded.

"Just doing our job. Let us take a look. Quick in and out."

The buzz sounded. The door clicked open.

Inside, the first guard barely had time to step back before he was cuffed. The second came in minutes later and froze. Same treatment.

"This is a robbery," one of the men said.

No shouting. No gunplay. No masks.

In 81 minutes, they moved like ghosts. Deliberate, from room to room.

They took thirteen works. Cut from frames. Vermeer, Rembrandt, Manet. The frames were left behind, like open mouths.

They left the guards in the basement, bound and dazed, then slipped back into the night. No one saw them or the art again.

CHAPTER 2

THE SANDPIPER HOTEL & CASINO

Atlantic City, 1998

THE Sandpiper Hotel and Casino wasn't the newest on the Atlantic City boardwalk; the hotel had a quiet elegance that appealed to men like Christopher Willoughby—old-money types, ivy-educated, and fraying at the edges. Its dark wood paneling and amber lighting reminded him of the club lounges in Philadelphia, which his father once ruled like a Roman senator.

That night, he met KiKi in the lobby bar. She wore a clingy black dress and heels that made her legs look endless. She smelled like jasmine and trouble.

They drank bourbon. She laughed at his jokes. He shared stories about boarding school, his job, and the pressure of expected greatness. She listened, or appeared to, her hand resting lightly on his thigh.

In the suite, she slowly undressed. Her body was gym-honed, dancer-flexible, and her eyes stayed fixed on his. She led him by the tie, unlooping it like a leash. They moved toward the bed in a slow-motion tangle of mouths and hands. He felt younger than he had in years—wanted, important. She whispered things he hadn't heard in years—maybe ever—and when she moaned his name, he believed her.

After she rolled off him and lit a cigarette, blowing the smoke toward the ceiling with bored elegance, he lay back, heart pounding. She looked over with a sleepy smile. "Next time," she said, "we should try something a little stronger."

That was how it started.

Their weekend encounters became a routine. Willoughby kept returning, and each time KiKi pushed the limits—more drinking, more drugs, rougher sex, less discretion. He told himself he was in control, but deep down he knew that wasn't true. She had him—hooked like the gamblers on the floors below.

By early summer, his losses were mounting. He had lost a hundred grand, maybe more, racked up across two casinos under a corporate line of credit he thought no one would ever trace. KiKi's tastes got pricier too. She talked about trips to St. Barts, a Cartier watch, coke cut with something smoother. He obliged. Eager to please. Afraid of losing her.

The night it all fell apart, he barely remembered the order of events.

There was champagne at dinner and more coke back in the suite. She wanted to play rough, but he wasn't in control of himself –his hands grabbing, pressure mounting. He remembered a shove, her voice sharp, then a blur. Darkness. Blackout.

When he woke, it was morning. Light spilled through the curtains like an interrogation lamp.

His mouth was dry. His head throbbed. He sat up –naked from

the waist down, body aching. His shirt hung off one shoulder, a button missing. His belt lay on the floor like a snake. He looked around, expecting KiKi.

But she wasn't there.

A man sat in the upholstered chair near the window, half in shadow.

He wore a charcoal overcoat over a dark suit, a fedora pulled low. A fat cigar burned in his hand, the tip glowing red as he took a long draw and exhaled smoke toward the ceiling.

"Well, well. Sleeping Beauty finally wakes up."

Willoughby bolted upright. "Who the hell are you?"

"Relax, counselor. I'm the cleanup crew. You're welcome, by the way."

"What are you talking about? How'd you get in here?"

The man grinned without humor. "You don't remember much, huh? That's what coke and premium single malt will do to you."

"Where's KiKi?"

"She's fine. Well, not fine –got a nasty bruise on her head, cracked her face on the nightstand when things got a little outta hand. Some blood on the carpet. She's got a story to tell, too. One that don't end well for you."

"I never laid a hand on her!" Willoughby snapped.

The man stood. Slowly. Deliberately. He walked to the bed and dropped a stack of Polaroids on the comforter. "Then maybe you can explain these."

The first photo showed KiKi face down on the carpet, half-naked, blood across her temple and shoulder. Another showed her back—welted and red. A third was of Willoughby, unconscious, with his shirt torn and a smear of blood across his chest.

Willoughby's throat dried. "This is a setup."

"No shit." The man pulled another drag from the cigar. "You think we let a goose like you waddle around unplucked?"

"What do you want?" Willoughby asked, voice now low, tinged with resignation.

The man leaned in, his tone more sinister.

"You owe the Sandpiper a hundred large. Plus, interest. And the girl? She wants hush money. Ten grand might buy her silence. Maybe."

Willoughby looked down at the photos again, disbelief morphing into panic. "If this gets out…"

"It won't. Not if you play ball." The stranger dropped his cigar into the empty room service glass and watched it hiss out. "My boss wants a lawyer. Quiet type. Someone who knows how to keep numbers moving and his nose clean. You fit the bill."

"I can't be involved with…" Willoughby faltered.

"With who? Guys who helped you keep your secret last night. Or guys who'll bury you if this hits the cops?"

The man stepped closer. "Think of this as… a retainer. You're on the payroll now. Maybe we ask you to file some papers. Move some money. No big deal."

"And if I say no?"

"You won't."

The man tipped his hat, his smile thin and sharp as a switchblade.

"Clean yourself up, counselor. Go home, kiss your wife, tell her the meeting went well. You'll hear from us when we need you."

He paused at the door.

"Oh, and counselor? Welcome to the family."

He disappeared into the hallway, the lock clicking quietly behind him.

Willoughby sat on the edge of the bed, body trembling, a chill crawling up his spine. He looked at the photos again, then at the mirror.

His reflection stared back—rumpled, bloodied, broken.

And now… owned.

CHAPTER 3

THE DEBT IS CALLED

A precisely 11:00 a.m., the elevator doors parted, and Anthony "Sonny" Patrilla stepped into the marble lobby of Simon & Kershaw. He wore a tailored sharkskin suit with just enough shine to signal new money, a silk burgundy tie knotted with precision, and a white shirt so crisp it looked like it could cut paper. He moved like a man who expected doors to open—because they always did.

Two men flanked him, heavyset and stone-faced. One wore mirrored sunglasses indoors, while the other chewed gum as if it owed him money.

The receptionist, a junior paralegal in her second week, froze for a beat before rising. "Mr. Willoughby is expecting you," she said, voice barely above a whisper. Her eyes lingered on Sonny. His smile was smooth but stopped short of his eyes.

"Thank you, sweetheart," he said, flashing teeth too perfect to be kind.

Willoughby was pacing when the knock came. He straightened his tie, wiped his sweaty palms on his trousers, and opened the door.

"Mr. Patrilla. A pleasure." His voice cracked, just slightly.

Sonny walked in like he owned the place and didn't mind proving it. He ignored the desk and made straight for the leather couch, sitting with the relaxed sprawl of a man who had never been told no. The two enforcers stayed by the door, their bulk making the room feel two sizes smaller.

"Coffee, gentlemen?" Willoughby offered.

"We're good," Sonny said. "Let's get to it, Counselor."

Willoughby sat, throat dry.

Sonny reached into his inner pocket and produced a folded check. "Fifty grand retainer. Upfront. I'm told you're very good. I've got a few things that need handling—investments, trusts, property transfers. Discreet stuff. You understand."

He held out the check but didn't release it. "Course, this is just paperwork. You and I—we go back already."

Willoughby didn't answer. The room held its breath.

Sonny leaned in, eyes locked. "You remember the Sandpiper, Atlantic City? Two years ago. You and that little piece of tail, KiKi? Or maybe you don't. Hard to recall things with that much blow in your system, huh?"

Willoughby's mouth moved, but no words came.

"He was the guy in the chair." Sonny Patrilla motioned to Frankie Dellaro. "The Polaroids. You remember now?"

Frankie Dellaro snorted. The other heavy cracked his knuckles.

"I... I thought that was taken care of," Willoughby finally managed.

Sonny's smile turned cold. "It was. By me. You think that kind of cleanup comes free? That debt is due."

"I didn't know who you were," Willoughby said. "I didn't know this would come back—."

"Of course you didn't," Sonny said. "That's what makes you useful. And what makes you mine."

He dropped the check on the desk. It landed like a gavel.

"Sign the retainer agreement. Bring your firm into the fold. Legitimate legal services. That's all we're asking. No bodies. No guns. Just paper. Numbers. Things you already do."

Willoughby shifted in his seat. Sweat darkened his collar.

"And if I say no?"

Sonny tilted his head. "Then you and I get to see what happens when those Polaroids hit the inboxes at your firm. Maybe the local press, too. You're a partner, right? That means PR risk. Liability. A problem for a lot of people, mostly you."

He leaned in closer. "Or maybe someone finds KiKi's body floating near Barnegat Bay. Real shame. There are people and records who can put you together at the hotel, multiple times. Counselor, that's a story with legs. Guilty verdict or not, you're done."

Willoughby swallowed hard. "You'd go that far?"

Sonny's voice dropped to a whisper. "You don't get it. I already went that far. You're just catching up."

The silence that followed was broken only by the low tick of the antique clock on Willoughby's bookshelf.

Willoughby reached for the check.

"That's more like it," Sonny said. "Smart man. You just made a great career decision."

The document was drawn up within the hour. A clean, professional agreement between Simon & Kershaw and Mr.

Anthony Patrilla for general legal counsel and financial services. No different than any other high-net-worth client. On paper.

Sonny signed it with a flourish. "You just made your first deal with the devil, Counselor. Don't worry. He tips."

As they left, Sonny turned once more at the door. "Oh, and one more thing. You won't be working alone. I hear there's a guy on your team named Manetti. Mike Manetti. Real wizard with accounts. I want him looped in. Use him as your buffer. Clean hands for you, counselor."

Willoughby nodded, dazed. "Of course."

"You'll hear from us."

The door clicked shut. Willoughby leaned back in his chair, heart pounding. His gaze drifted to the framed photo of his wife on the bookshelf. Her smile seemed farther away than ever.

In that moment, Christopher Willoughby realized something chilling: The past doesn't bury itself. It sends people like Sonny to collect.

CHAPTER 4

THE BRONX THREAD

MIKE Manetti didn't have the pedigree. No Ivy League crest. No bloodline traced to old money or founding families. What he had was grit, and Wallace saw that early.

Manetti grew up three flights above a corner bodega in the Bronx, as the only son of Sam and Louise Manetti. Sam worked at the Armitage Foundry, a block from the elevated train, shoveling sand and pouring steel into the blast furnaces—five days a week, fifty weeks a year. A union man. A Vietnam vet. Quiet and proud. He believed in this country the way you believe in family—you stick with it, even when it lets you down.

Their two-bedroom walk-up shook when trucks went by. Mike shared a room with his younger sister, Andrea, and learned early how to tune out the world. He was good with numbers. Better with people. Ran poker nights in the park by sixteen. Knew how to read a man's face, not just his hand.

He made his first real money at the Aqueduct racetrack, collecting tips for bets and betting against irregular spreads. A bookmaker once told Wallace that the kid had math in his fingertips.

That caught Wallace's attention.

James L. Wallace operated the Gentle Brush Car Wash on Boston Road, but that was a cover. The real cash came from metal—specifically, scrap from the costume jewelry trade. Refinery work. Wallace knew how to skim a percentage of gold and keep it off the books. Legal enough to avoid the feds' radar. Shady enough to require loyal help.

Wallace brought Manetti into the car wash, then moved him to the back office of the refinery, handing him a clipboard and an opportunity. The boy paid attention, quick with numbers, quiet about secrets, and didn't need to be told twice.

By the time Manetti was a high school senior, he was managing refinery accounts, monitoring the weight differences on incoming scrap, and overseeing the sale of refined metals into gray-market channels. Wallace liked him. More than that, he trusted him.

When Manetti talked about law school, Wallace didn't laugh. He helped him get there—making quiet cash payments to cover expenses, writing a letter to a judge who chaired the law school's alumni board, and calling a state senator from Queens.

New England Law School awarded Manetti a need-based scholarship. He graduated with a B average and no debt. Passed the bar on his first attempt.

Wallace, who had run for borough president twice and lost each time, had connections. One of them was Chase Montgomery, the white-haired managing partner of Simon & Kershaw, an old Manhattan firm that valued legacy, discretion, and the illusion of ethical purity.

Wallace arranged lunch for just the two of them, him and

Montgomery. Montgomery was skeptical at first—he didn't care much for Bronx accents or public-school law degrees—but Wallace strongly vouched for the kid. He said the kid had talent, a good feel for numbers, and discretion. Wallace smiled the way men do when they mean something more.

Montgomery gave Manetti a six-month contract in the Financial Planning Department.

The man who led that department, Christopher Willoughby, saw Manetti as useful protection. Willoughby, born on the Philadelphia Main Line, had neither backbone nor sharp intellect. But he inherited connections, the kind with sizable portfolios and a preference for discreet dealings. He kept his job by making introductions and approving transactions he didn't fully understand. Manetti, however, understood everything.

By year two, Manetti was creating complex setups—LLCs tucked inside offshore trusts, shadow partnerships, land deals using art as collateral. The kind of paperwork that made tracking assets take years and often led nowhere. Perfect for hiding assets.

Willoughby watched, impressed and quietly unnerved. Manetti worked like a man with something to prove. Or something to hide.

Wallace faded from the picture after a minor stroke, but he had done his part. Manetti was embedded, trusted, liked—especially by clients who needed discreet work that couldn't be discussed in conference calls.

What Willoughby didn't know—what he suspected but never voiced—was that Wallace's referral came with hidden strings. Strings not immediately obvious.

When Sonny Patrilla came calling, they wanted Manetti on the books. Willoughby might have opened the door, but it was Manetti they trusted.

And that's how a boy from the Bronx, who collected gold dust sweepings off a refinery floor, ended up laundering fortunes through a firm that once served a sitting president.

He never forgot the weight of that. Not in New York. Not in exile.

CHAPTER 5

THE MORNING OF

Tuesday, September 11, 2001 – 6:45 a.m.
Lexington Avenue, Manhattan

THE radio clicked alive with a soft crackle. Marvin Gaye's voice drifted through the static, smooth and soulful.

Michael Manetti opened one eye, then the other. Sheets were tangled at his waist. The other side of the bed was empty. Cool to the touch.

She was gone.

Sunlight slanted through the shutters, cutting the hardwood floor into bars of gold and shadow. His wrinkled Oxford shirt still hung over the chair from last night. For a moment, he stayed still. Just lay there, breathing, letting the quiet stretch out longer than it should.

Then he swung his legs over the edge of the mattress.

His shoulders ached from the weekend. Spring Lake was worth it. Off the grid, no calls from the firm, no questions from clients. Just Sally, the surf, and a few hours of honesty he would never admit he craved. He'd left her at her apartment last night—safest that way.

Firm rules were clear: no entanglements with staff. She knew it too. But rules don't warm your skin.

He stepped into the shower, turned the water hot, and let it burn away salt air, lingering guilt, and the tenderness he didn't want to feel. He shaved slowly, steam fogging the mirror, towel around his waist. He studied his reflection: lean, tanned, sharp-eyed. Success hung off him like armor, and he needed it that way.

Manetti dressed carefully. Navy pinstripe suit, pale blue shirt, yellow tie knotted tightly. Gold cufflinks, Rolex on his wrist, shoes polished to a mirror finish. He packed his Montblanc briefcase— Zurich contracts, a memo from Willoughby, notes from a steel magnate in Hamburg that smelled off. He flagged it for later. Hamburg always meant shadows.

The apartment door locked behind him with a click.

Downstairs, the doorman nodded. "Morning, Mr. Manetti."

"Looks like it," Manetti replied.

Outside, the city pulsed. Early fall, air crisp as linen. Vendors stacked paper cups and poured coffee that steamed like smoke from manholes. Commuters pushed forward, faces set. Summer vacations a memory. New York moved as if it could never be stopped.

A black Lincoln town car slid to the curb like it knew him.

"World Trade Centre, Church Street," he said, sliding into the leather seat.

The driver nodded. No words.

Manetti leaned back, watching Broadway blur past. Canal Street. Chambers. The skyline grew taller as they headed south. The twin towers jutted into the blue sky like monuments to permanence.

He reached into his briefcase and thumbed open his Day-Timer.

Handwritten notes, offshore codes, names. Insurance. Reminders of the life he kept on the edge of a knife. Secrets that could destroy entire empires. He jotted down a thought, closed it, then tucked it away.

The phone buzzed once. Unknown number. He let it die in his pocket.

The Lincoln braked at Vesey and Church.

He handed the driver a twenty and stepped out.

The plaza spread before him, alive with early morning suits, tourists craning their necks, vendors hawking bagels. Above, the towers soared into the endless blue. Mythical. Invulnerable. Permanent.

He adjusted his tie, briefcase firm in his hand. He didn't realize it yet, but this was the last morning of the world he knew – his final walk through those revolving glass doors.

In less than two hours, permanence would turn to dust. And Michael Manetti would disappear with it.

CHAPTER 6

ONE WORLD TRADE CENTER

North Tower

One World Trade Center 76th Floor – Simon & Kershaw

MICHAEL Manetti stepped out of the town car and walked across the plaza, carrying a Montblanc briefcase. The September sky was clear and blue—so vivid it looked painted. The towers reflected it back, with glass and steel that seemed invincible and eternal.

Inside, the North Tower lobby hummed with commuter energy—security guards, vendors, employees boarding elevators, voices rising and falling with the rhythm of another Manhattan morning.

On the 76th floor of Simon & Kershaw's executive offices, the marble lobby was polished to a museum gloss. The firm had always taken pride in its appearance.

The nameplate on the frosted glass wall gleamed: SIMON & KERSHAW LLP. Founded in the 1950s by two Army vets who clawed their way through public law schools on the GI Bill, the firm was built on sweat, grit, and the dreams of first-generation professionals. They grew into a midtown powerhouse, positioning themselves as champions of the working entrepreneur, and they thrived during the city's post-war **boom**. But by the late '90s, that bootstrap mentality had hardened into arrogance, reflected in the clientele and makeup of its personnel. The office floors were still mostly filled with white men in tailored suits, their jokes often chauvinistic, their camaraderie more country-club than collegial.

Manetti wasn't from old money. He was more like the founders. He lacked prep school connections or a family name that opened doors. But Simon & Kershaw still valued something else—he was hungry, ruthless with numbers, and willing to take on the jobs newer associates wouldn't touch. That made him indispensable.

"Good morning, Mr. Manetti," Betty at reception said, her smile polite but tight, the way women here often smiled when they felt watched.

"Morning, Betty," he said, already moving.

His heels clicked loudly against the marble as he passed cubicles and glass offices. He spotted Sally rounding a corner—sharp navy dress, heels that matched her ambition. She carried herself like she belonged wherever she wanted to be.

"You look rested," she said with a teasing smile.

He grinned. "I am."

She laughed softly and quickly, but her eyes stayed a bit too long. Then they discreetly shifted away, each heading in different directions.

His office was near the corner. It smelled faintly of fresh flowers and leather. The desk was spotless—Jane Sampson, his administrative assistant, helped him keep it that way; a compartmentalized life in a room of glass. A stack of files waited, with the morning sun casting stripes on the carpet into rectangles.

He didn't plan to stay long. He had an early off-site at the coffee shop in the South Tower—a meeting with Ralph Collucci, his childhood friend from The Bronx, whom he introduced into the professional circle of a client, Anthony "Sonny" Patrilla, a New York mobster. Collucci was an accountant, the kind of guy who could balance books in one hand and buy an auditor with the other. Manetti never met him in the office; too many eyes here, too close a connection with a controversial client.

Manetti pulled a file from the drawer. The red sticker read: *Usher*—one of the Patrilla laundering schemes. The numbers were starting to scream, too heavy, too obvious. Even he knew the pattern was overdue for a collapse.

He tucked the file into his briefcase, straightened his tie, and left his office for the elevator.

In the lobby, the elevator to his left dinged.

He watched two men step out, dressed in dark suits with calm eyes. A glint of a gold badge reflected off one man's belt. He heard receptionist Betty's voice from around the partition.

"Gentlemen, can I help you?"

FBI. It hit him like a shot.

He moved smoothly through the corridor, away from reception, heading toward the south elevator bank with his briefcase in hand.

******

"Special Agents Turci and Alves, FBI," one said, flipping his I.D. toward the receptionist.

"We're here to see Michael Manetti."

Betty blinked. "I think he left earlier, but I'll check with his assistant."

Jane Sampson, his administrative assistant, appeared at the partition, hair pulled back, crisp blouse. "I'm Mr. Manetti's assistant. He's off-site this morning. How can I help you?"

"When's he expected back?" Turci asked.

"Before lunch, I believe."

"We'll wait," he said. Agent Turci settled into a chair with a line of sight down the hallway. His partner Alves walked to the hospitality table, poured a coffee, took a Danish, a napkin, and positioned a chair across from Turci.

Jane returned to her desk. Her fingers trembled just slightly as she picked up the phone.

******

Manetti had crossed the plaza and rode the South Tower escalator down to the concourse. The mall was already bustling—coffee carts hissing steam, the smell of bagels in the air, cell phones pressed to ears. He moved in sync with the flow of pedestrians through the shopping area.

He didn't know what the Feds wanted. But he had guesses.

He didn't know it yet, but the sky above the city was about to fall.

CHAPTER 7

THE FAULT LINE

Concourse – South Tower, WTC

THE coffee shop was on the Concourse level, tucked in a corner near the elevators. No sunlight or street sounds reached this deep. The air smelled like burnt toast and coffee.

Ralph Collucci sat in the back booth. Chesterfield in one hand, coffee in the other. He was sweating already.

Mike Manetti spotted him from across the room. Same old Ralph — balding, hunched, tie askew like a crooked apology. He slid into the seat across from Collucci.

"Ralphie."

"Mike. Jesus. We've got trouble."

"I got that from your message."

Ralph took a drag. Exhaled slowly.

"It's the Feds. Two agents came to see me Friday."

"What did they ask?"

"About Patrilla. About our connection. But then one said something that froze me — *Usher*. They asked about Usher," Ralph said with emphasis.

Manetti's face didn't change, but something behind his eyes locked down.

"That operation's airtight," he said. "Five years in the Caymans. Every transfer buttoned up. No glitches. That bank manager's been on the payroll longer than my barber."

"Someone's talking," Ralph said. "Or the Feds have something. I've been sweating it all weekend."

"You file clean tax returns for the legit side, right?"

"Of course. But Mike, they're digging. Deep. I'm afraid a subpoena is coming."

A waitress stepped over, pot in hand.

"More coffee, hon?"

Manetti nodded. She poured a cup. Ralph waved her off.

She moved to the next table. Her name tag read Hazel, with a flower pinned to her lapel. Her hair was lacquered and stubbornly styled, a remnant from her days at Horn & Hardart.

When she left, Ralph leaned in.

"I'm not just worried about the Feds. It's Sonny. If he thinks I'm a weak link..."

"You're not."

"But if he thinks I am... I've got a wife, Mike. Two kids. What if he—?"

"He won't," Manetti said. "You've been loyal. Careful."

"But they don't care. Perceptions are enough. If I'm subpoenaed and have to testify, I'd be a threat, just like you would be, Mike. We have to be careful, very careful," Collucci continued, "that's what I wanted to tell you so you can be prepared."

Ralph lit another cigarette with shaking hands.

"We need a plan," he said. "A real one."

Before Manetti could answer, his phone rang.

"Mike, this is Jane," her voice crackled through his phone. "There are two FBI agents here to see you."

"Where are they now?"

"Waiting in reception. I told them you'd be back before lunch."

"Good."

He hung up. His eyes drifted to Ralph.

"They're already at my office."

Ralph's lips parted, but he didn't speak.

It was 8:46 a.m. when the floor trembled.

The air snapped.

The lights flickered across the concourse. The building groaned. A ceramic mug slid off a table and shattered onto the floor.

The ground heaved once. Then again.

An old man, leaving the men's room, fell sideways to the floor. Someone screamed. Somewhere, more glass broke.

Silence followed. The air thickened with uncertainty.

Then a low murmur spread through the concourse. People stopped walking and turned to each other, seeking reassurance. Asking and looking up toward the ceiling as if expecting it to fall.

Hazel clutched the coffee pot.

"What the hell?"

The noise outside was not reaching them. No sirens. No shouting, Not yet.

"I felt a **boom**," someone said. "Like a big one."

"Was it a gas main?" said another.

"Could be an earthquake," said Manetti. "Or maybe a train derailment."

"Or maybe it was a bomb," Hazel whispered. "Like last time."

People began to gather by the escalators. The air felt off. Suddenly still.

Manetti turned and looked toward the concourse elevators. People were confused but resumed moving—commuters, tourists, and businessmen in suits.

Everything looked normal for a moment.

But it wasn't.

Manetti's jaw clenched. He turned to Ralph.

"They know," he said.

"What?"

"The Feds. They're not just poking. They're here. And this..."

He didn't finish the sentence.

The sound was approaching now. Soft. Echoing. Menacing. The pressure was mounting.

And somewhere inside him, he felt it:

The fault line had cracked.

CHAPTER 8

ASHFALL

The rumble had passed, but the fear had not.

PEOPLE began talking again. Initially quiet, then louder and more agitated. Voices grew louder behind the coffee shop's walls. Then, beyond that. Then everywhere.

It was no longer a tremor. It was panic.

People were running, some toward the escalators from the train platforms. One woman screamed as she fled down the corridor, her briefcase left behind.

Hazel hurried back to the booth.

"I just heard," she said, breathless. "Someone said a plane hit the North Tower. A big one. Flames coming out of the windows high up. Debris. People falling!"

"Falling?" Ralph said, pale.

"From the windows," Hazel answered.

Manetti looked toward the corridor. The stream of people was growing thicker.

"If it was a small plane, like back in '45—the Empire State Building—damage, sure. But it's stayed standing," Ralph offered.

Manetti shook his head. "A small plane doesn't drop bodies from a hundred stories up."

The coffee shop's old wall-mounted television flickered, and a sharp tone echoed from the tinny speakers. At 8:48 a.m., a red banner scrolled across the TV screen: **Special News Bulletin**.

A traffic chopper's view showed the North Tower—black smoke pouring out the side 90 stories up.

"...video feed coming in from Air Traffic Copters... smoke rising from the upper floors of the North Tower at the World Trade Center in Lower Manhattan... multiple reports of an aircraft impact, possibly a large passenger plane..."

Hazel gasped. "Jesus, Mary, and Joseph..."

Manetti took his cell out of his pocket and dialed Jane's number. The call went straight to voicemail. "Jane, it's Mike. Call me."

He dialed Sally, no answer. Left the same voicemail message.

Crowds flooded the concourse of the South Tower—running, shouting, panicking. Some hurried toward the Liberty Street exit. Others headed to 4 World Trade Center and Church Street. Many were just trying to figure out which way was out.

The elevator banks hissed open. Suits and secretaries poured into the lower level, coughing, screaming, some crying.

Above, the windows of Building Two, the South Tower, revealed a view of the horror next door—black smoke billowing from the gash, fire flashing behind glass. People in the South Tower froze, staring, as silhouettes waved shirts from broken windows across the plaza, desperate and trapped.

At 8:56 a.m., the South Tower building-wide public address system clicked on:

"Ladies and gentlemen, Building Two is secure. There is no need to evacuate. You may return to your offices."

People blinked. Hazel crossed herself.

"Bullshit," Manetti muttered.

A few minutes later, it came again.

"Situation occurred in Building One (North Tower). If conditions warrant, you may begin an orderly evacuation of Building Two."

"Ralph," Mike said, standing fast. "We're getting out of here."

They headed for the elevators—but stopped.

"No," Manetti said, looking up. "Take the escalator."

He turned and grabbed Ralph's arm.

Then the world shook again.

9:03 a.m.

Impact – South Tower

It was different this time. Deeper. Meaner.

United Airlines Flight 175, a Boeing 767, departed from Logan Airport at 8:14 a.m. bound for Los Angeles with 51 passengers and 9 crew members, and crashed into the South Tower at 9:03.

The building jolted, followed by a roaring sound unlike anything survivors had heard before. Metal tore apart like paper. Jet fuel flowed and burned like lava. Air rushed at velocities meant for the open sky, not trapped inside a steel tower.

A shockwave roared through the elevator shafts. Flames, dust, and debris chased it. A tornado of noise, heat, and wind.

Elevator doors exploded outward.

With each elevator crashing into the lobby, another wave of smoke, steel, and flame surged into the concourse—carrying people with it.

Mike and Ralph were on the Concourse when a blast from a falling elevator knocked them backward. They hit the floor hard—people, chairs, glass—all crashing together. Then came silence. But it wasn't quiet; it was deafening—a vacuum in the air and collapsed lungs.

Manetti opened his mouth. Nothing. Dust filled it.

He blinked into a world that was no longer a world. Just shadow and ash.

He looked for Ralph. Reached for him.

"Ralph—!"

No answer.

He couldn't even hear his own voice.

Then, nearby in the darkness, a woman screamed for help.

Manetti crawled toward the sound.

Glass tore at his hands. He found her. Felt her body—small, trembling.

"I've got you," he said, unsure if she could hear. "We're getting out."

The lights were gone. The chandeliers were gone. The sunlight was gone.

The ceiling cracked again, and plaster rained down. Another elevator collapsed, and doors burst open. Wires sparked and hissed.

Manetti helped her stand.

"Hold onto me."

They stumbled ahead through darkness. Each step took faith. One step, then a stumble as he moved with the women on his arm. Then another.

Voices. A beam from a flashlight. A man in turnout gear.

"Over here!" Mike shouted.

A firefighter rushed toward them. "We've got an opening."

He assisted the woman through a broken window. Mike helped two others.

He shouted back: "Over here! There's a way out!"

More bodies appeared from the darkness. Bleeding. Dust-covered. Some barefoot. Moaning.

Mike helped push them through.

Once it was clear, he pulled himself through the window.

9:35 a.m. – Outside

The air was thick and gray. Nothing but grayness everywhere. No sky, only smoke and dust.

The sun had vanished.

Sirens wailed through the clouds. Radios crackled with static. Firefighters shouted into megaphones that few could hear.

Mike stumbled across the sidewalk, dropping his briefcase as he moved toward the street. A cloud of dust rose to the sky, further blocking the sun. On the street, as the cloud rose it also expanded on the ground, engulfing everything in its path. Manetti took shelter beneath a brown package delivery van to escape the oncoming cloud. Watching the cloud move quickly reminded him of the early 1950s disaster movies featuring atomic-bred monsters overtaking a city.

He curled up, covering his face. Breathing dust, his chest heaved. Covered in ash.

The city was breaking apart around him.

And then—

9:59 a.m. – Collapse

The sound came from above. Then from everywhere.

The South Tower tilted slightly, just enough.

Then it fell.

Floor by floor, it collapsed downward, folding on itself like an accordion. Five hundred million tons of concrete, steel, and glass plummeted, destroying everything in its path. Concrete turned to dust. Steel, softened by intense heat, bent and twisted.

Mike watched it disappear.

Ten seconds.

That's all it took.

Twenty-nine minutes later, at 10:28 a.m., the North Tower, housing the firm and the souls of Simon & Kershaw, collapsed. Everything was gone.

CHAPTER 9

THE TWIN TOWERS

The smoke didn't stop for days.
And the silence—when it came—was worse
than the sound.

OWER Manhattan was cordoned off. Block by block, barricades
went up. Sirens kept blaring. Then they ceased. Then the digging
started.

For weeks, trucks rolled along the West Side Highway hauling
twisted beams and powdered glass lifted by steel-jawed mechanical
monsters at Ground Zero. Debris from the towers once known as
the center of world finance, now just weight.

They hauled it to Staten Island, to the landfill. That's where
the sifting started.

What they didn't find on the streets, they searched for in the
ash—bone fragments, wallets, wedding rings, a piece of a company
ID, bits and pieces of lives.

The news didn't let up. Not for months.

Nearly 3000 dead.

343 firefighters. 37 Port Authority officers. 23 NYPD officers

and detectives.

Two FBI agents, last seen on the 76th floor of the North Tower, were casualties.

One of them was named Turci, and the other was Alves.

Their badges were found. Nothing else.

Posters went up quickly. Missing faces tacked to barricades and utility poles—an international group of sons, daughters, secretaries, and janitors. Smiling in vacation shots, grinning from wedding pictures, staring from graduation portraits, holding diplomas and dreams.

Could they be somewhere in a hospital? Disoriented? Amnesiac? Maybe underground, waiting for rescue.

The hope faded with each passing hour and each passing day.

Then came the funerals—hundreds of them, sometimes four on one block. Bagpipes playing. Empty caskets. Folded flags.

The list of the missing kept growing even as it was shrinking.

CHAPTER 10

THE APARTMENT

Evening, September 11th
Upper East Side, Manhattan

B Y dusk on the 11th, the smoke still crept through the streets. A haze of ash floated from the south, quietly staining everything.

Mike Manetti moved through the gray like a ghost.

He didn't know how many hours had passed. Didn't care. Dust clung to his suit like a second skin, his tie had long been discarded, and his face was smeared with gray. He walked past shop windows without seeing, crossed streets against signals. Each step felt like a weight of coming reckoning.

The law was coming. The Bureau would discover the accounts, the shell companies, and the trails they left behind. They'd review Simon & Kershaw's client lists and see his name marked in offshore transactions and freeport contracts. There would be subpoenas and interrogations. Maybe more. Ralph's warning echoed in his mind—"loose ends."

He could see it. Some back room in a federal building. A bad deal. Or a parking garage with a silenced pistol. If the feds didn't get him, the Patrilla family would.

He walked past a storefront with a TV flickering in the window. A replay of the second plane hitting the tower played on the screen. People stood frozen, watching the loop. Their faces hollow.

He stopped, breathing shallow.

This wasn't just tragedy.

It was cover.

Everyone else was trying to make sense of what they had lost—loved ones, coworkers, friends. But Mike Manetti had lost something else: his life as he knew it. And maybe that wasn't the worst thing. Maybe it was a window, like the one he used to exit the tower.

If everyone believed he was gone...

His heart thudded once, heavy and cold. There was no going back. Not to the firm. Not to the man he was when the sun rose that morning. That man was already ashes.

He turned off Lexington and slipped into a small park, sat on a bench beneath a soot-covered maple, and let his thoughts settle. He needed time to breathe. To step outside the blast radius of what came next.

This tragedy, this unimaginable devastation, had cracked the world open. In the chaos, people would go missing. Records would blur. Bodies would never be recovered.

What if one of them was him?

He didn't need forever—just enough time to decide if there was any way back or only forward into the unknown. If he played it right, he could beat the odds, like he had done his whole life.

That was the moment it began.

Not with a disguise, but with a decision—a man walking alone through a burning city, choosing to vanish.

Mike Manetti would disappear to survive.

To outlast the fire.

To make something right.

Or at least, to try.

******

He reached his building on Lexington and 78th just after 9:00 p.m.

The uniformed doorman stood at the front, talking to another tenant. Too much risk. Mike circled the block and watched the service entrance.

Back here, there were no doormen—just steel doors and graffiti. The door was locked, as expected. He waited in the shadows near the trash cans. Motionless. Eyes on the door.

Ten, maybe fifteen minutes passed. Then, luck.

A teenager stepped out — holding a pizza box in one hand and a flip phone in the other. Left the door propped open with a stick. Didn't look back.

Manetti slipped inside.

The stairwell reeked of bleach and cigarettes. He bypassed the elevator and climbed the stairs, six flights, his breathing even, his footsteps silent.

He reached his floor. The back hallway was quiet. He turned the pantry key and slipped in.

No lights.

He knew the layout. He didn't need them.

The apartment was just as he had left it: coffee mug in the sink, newspaper on the kitchen table. The city's last normal morning was frozen in time.

The answering machine blinked red.

Three messages.

He pressed play. Andrea, his sister, her voice cracked through the speaker.

"Mike, it's me. Please call. I've been trying all day. Are you okay?"

Second message. Same voice, more frantic.

"I saw the news. I don't know what's happening. Please, God— call me."

Third message, softer.

"I don't know if you're alive. But if you are, I love you."

The light stopped blinking.

He stood there a long moment, just breathing, thinking.

Then he moved.

******

In the bathroom, behind the cabinet mirror, there was a loose panel. He popped it open. Behind it, a Manila envelope wrapped in plastic—flash drives and documents inside.

He pulled it out.

Inside were the files and his insurance.

Client names, bank affiliations, transaction lists, passwords, routing codes, offshore corporations with names inspired by mythology, literature, and astrology—creative and easy to remember.

If he was going to survive an investigation or retribution, this envelope was the life raft.

In the bedroom closet, beneath a stack of shoe boxes, he found the duffel bag. A go-bag. Cash. Passport. Dopp kit. A pre-paid phone wrapped in socks. Clothes. A backup laptop.

Manetti took one last look around the apartment, checking for anything out of place. Satisfied, he left it as it was — dishes in the sink, towel still damp from his last shower. Let them believe he never came back.

He left the same way he entered. No one saw him.

******

Back at Lexington, he crossed the avenue and disappeared into the night.

He didn't know where he was going. Only that he wouldn't be back soon, or ever.

He was a dead man now.

CHAPTER 11

WAKING IN NEW ORLEANS

THE early Fall light came in hard through the window facing Bayou Street. It caught the edge of the bedspread where Manetti still lay, fully dressed, half-dreaming, half-remembering.

The hum of the old A/C droned. Somewhere below, a trash truck clanged and shook a steel bin. Then came sharp beeps as it backed away. The city returned to stillness.

He hadn't moved much in hours.

Two windows. One to the street, one to the alley. One for escape. One for shadow.

His shirt was still wrinkled. Blood and dust still smeared the cuffs. He hadn't shaved in days. His eyes puffy. His mouth dry.

The room reeked of stale smoke and mildew, the kind of place meant for people on the run or on the edge.

He didn't know which one he was yet.

Three days blurred past him. New York to Jersey, Jersey to D.C., then south. Bus stations and toilets that didn't flush. Fast food and cold coffee. Too many faces. None that mattered.

The Nashville Greyhound terminal was noisy. He stared at the tote board as if it had answers.

New Orleans — Dock 3
Departing 10:15 p.m.

******

Today, he sat on the edge of the hotel bed in New Orleans, with the same wrinkled navy suit. Tie gone. Collar open. A Wall Street ghost.

His beard itched. His back ached. He needed a shower, a razor, a meal, and a plan.

He looked down at his hands. Dirt under the nails. Dust still in the cuffs of his pants.

His Wall Street uniform — ruined. He didn't care. It helped him disappear.

By the time the bus reached Louisiana, no one noticed him.

A man in a wrinkled suit. Three-day beard. Eyes dead from somewhere up north.

Could've been anyone.

Could've been no one.

And that's what he needed to be.

******

The hallway outside Room 203 was quiet. Dim. One low-watt bulb near the end. Paint peeling like skin. It smelled of despair.

Downstairs, the clerk sat behind the tall counter, deeply sunk in an upholstered chair, watching news roll in on a nine-inch TV. Eyes hollow.

"Hell of a thing happened," the old man muttered. "Them damn A-rabs."

Manetti said nothing.

"Mr. Smith, right?" the clerk said, scanning the ledger. "Came in late last night. Greyhound, huh?"

"Yeah."

"You hungry?"

"I could eat."

The clerk nodded toward the street. "Sun-Up Diner. Half a block."

Manetti dropped two quarters into the newspaper box on the sidewalk and pulled out a *USA Today*. The headline screamed across the front:

"A Nation Mourns: Day of Prayer Declared"

He folded it and walked past a man curled up, sleeping on the concrete. Same scene as back home, just different accents.

The smell of bacon and fried onions drifted out from the diner door.

Inside, a waitress wiped down a table. Two kids sat in a booth, eyes sunken. They didn't speak. Just stirred coffee and stared past each other.

A week ago, Manetti wouldn't have noticed them.

Today, he saw everything.

He sat at the counter. The man behind it was both chef and server. Tattoos covered his forearms. A pack of Camels was rolled up in his T-shirt sleeve. 'Semper Fi' was inked on his arm.

"What'll it be?"

"Two over, bacon crisp. Wheat toast. Black coffee."

The man nodded as he cracked the eggs on the grill.

"You don't look like you're from around here," he said over his shoulder.

"Why's that?"

"You got a neat haircut, shoes worth more than this diner. But you look like somebody who lost everything."

"I'm looking for a friend."

The cook lit a cigarette, turned to Manetti.

"Who?"

"Goes by the name Sailor. Used to run a tattoo parlor down by the river. Knew my father in the Army."

"Sailor?" He thought for a second. "Yeah, still around, I think. Shop's closed though, but I heard he lives upstairs. He rents a room on Water Street."

"Thanks."

"You military, too?"

"No. My father. Green Beret. Vietnam."

"He make it back?"

Manetti nodded. "Sort of."

That was enough. He understood. The cook slid the plate over and turned to another customer. Manetti ate quickly, left cash on the counter, and stepped out into the heat, following the cook's directions.

CHAPTER 12

THE LIFE THAT WASN'T

WATER Street was old brick and rust. The bones of a river neighborhood long past its prime. Warehouses with broken windows. Steel doors rusted shut. Everything sweating under a September sun and humidity.

He found the place—locked storefront, faded sign. Beside it, a door marked **Rooms for Rent**.

Upstairs, a woman sat by the window, smoking. She looked at him as if she'd seen a thousand ghosts. Tilted her head.

"Sailor here?" Manetti asked.

"Number three up the stairs," as she motioned with her chin.

The stairwell was dark. The floor creaked of dried wood.

The door was open.

Inside, a once-soldier and noted Gulf Coast tattoo icon, a thin man sat in a sun-cracked recliner. Bare feet. Wearing a New Orleans Saints T-shirt and boxers. Faded tattoos ran up his arms — bearded with a tired face.

"You Sailor?"

"Depends. Who's asking?"

"I'm Sam Manetti's kid. Mike."

Sailor squinted. Said nothing.

"You knew my dad. Vietnam. I met you once, years ago. You showed me your snakes."

Sailor looked at the aquariums. Lizards and snakes coiled in corners, eyes staring out.

"Your old man still breathing?"

"Not anymore."

"Figures."

Sailor leaned back. Lit a joint. Blew the smoke toward the ceiling fan.

"Why are you here?"

"I need help."

Sailor said nothing. Waited.

"I survived the Towers. I was there. I shouldn't be alive, but I am. And now, I'm a liability to people with long arms and short patience."

"Mob?"

"Clients. Maybe Feds." Manetti answered.

"Same thing."

Manetti sat on the wooden chair. It wobbled under his weight.

"I need a passport. New ID. Something that'll get me out clean. And back in, if needed. Right now, I just need to get away for a while, maybe to The Bahamas, Key West. Someplace I can be invisible."

Sailor cracked a knuckle.

"My hands ain't what they used to be."

"I don't have another option."

Sailor looked him over. Thought it through.

Then nodded once.

"A thousand bucks. No guarantees," he said.

"Ok. That's better than nothing."

"But first," Sailor added, grinding out the joint. "You're gonna need to go dig up a ghost."

Manetti blinked.

"I need you to find me a name. In the cemetery. Someone who died young. Clean record. Right age. No one likely to miss 'em."

Sailor's voice was flat.

"You want to disappear; you start by borrowing the dead."

CHAPTER 13

NAMES OF THE FORGOTTEN

THE gates moaned on rusted hinges, the kind of sound that carried old secrets and kept them.

Lafayette Cemetery stretched out in sun-bleached rows beneath a canopy of magnolia and cypress. Hot sunlight pierced through the branches. Shadows drifted over the gravestones like slow waves.

Mike Manetti stepped through the Prytania Street entrance and into another world.

Sailor had told him where to go. *Not the St. Louis Cemetery,* he'd said. *You want ghosts that stay buried. Go to Lafayette. Orphan section.*

So, he did.

The caretaker's office pointed him toward the back, Section K, labeled for the Home for Destitute Orphan Boys. A place that gathered the unwanted or lost, provided them shelter, and when the world was finished with them, carved their names in stone.

Manetti passed the crypts, passed the merchant families with their marble mausoleums, until he reached the stretch of narrow markers in the dirt. Many were crooked. Some unreadable. Most forgotten.

He walked slowly.

1964, 1970, 1968

A lot of boys died young here. Many with no known birthdates.

He knelt at a sunken slab and wiped the moss with his sleeve.

Toby Raymond Dupré
August 10, 1967 – April 2, 1978

Too early.

Another:
Andre Joseph Landry
Born 1969. Died 1982.

Then one that stopped him.

The headstone was barely visible. Covered in vines and dirt. He knelt again and used his hand to scrape it clear.

Elijah Dean Broussard
April 15, 1968 – May 25, 1980

Twelve years old.

Just dates. A clean one. One year off his own. Close enough to live inside.

Elijah wouldn't work. Not for a man like him. But Dean... Dean was good. And Broussard gave him just enough cover. French, Southern, adaptable. Add the "E." at the front, and it sounded polished. Uptown. Professional.

He wrote the details on a slip of paper, his hand trembling slightly due to the heat and humidity. The pen left smudges. Sweat dripped from his forehead onto the page. None of it mattered.

E. Dean Broussard.

Born 1968. Died 1980.

And now, reborn in 2001.

In the caretaker's office, he asked for more information on Broussard. He was directed to the card files under Section K, arranged alphabetically by name.

The index card contained the information Sailor needed: date of birth, mother's name Josephine Broussard, age 18, father: N/A, and place of birth in St. Charles Parish, Louisiana.

A red stamp read across the card: *Ward of the State of Louisiana.* Handwritten below, *April 18, 1968.*

He sat on a cracked concrete bench nearby. The air was still. The graves didn't speak, but they didn't have to.

So many boys.

So many names no longer said aloud.

And now he would carry one.

Manetti stared at the page and felt something he hadn't in days.

Guilt.

Not for taking the name. But for needing to.

He thought about all the bodies still buried beneath steel and concrete in Lower Manhattan. Names still being published. Faces in the newspapers.

He had survived by inches. By seconds. By luck. And now he was stealing the identity of a child who never saw fifteen.

He leaned back and looked up through the branches.

Maybe there was something to remember here. Something he hadn't figured out yet.

But he would.

CHAPTER 14

CALL TO ANDREA

BACK at the Bayou Street hotel, Manetti asked the clerk for a pay phone. Without looking up, the clerk jerked a thumb toward a dim corner near the vending machine.

He found it. A leftover from another decade. He dug for quarters, slotted them.

Ring. Ring.

Andrea picked up on the second.

"Hello?"

He swallowed once. Then:

"Andi. It's me."

Silence. Then a sharp inhale.

"Michael? Michael—My God! Where have you been? Are you okay? What happened to you?"

"I'm alright," he said. His voice was low and even. "I'm safe. That's all I can tell you."

"Where are you? Are you hurt?"

"I can't say. And no, not hurt."

"Michael, I— I thought you were dead. The law firm, the

towers—I saw everything on TV and couldn't reach you."

"I know," he said. "I know. Andi, listen to me. I need your help."

There was a pause. Her breathing slowed, trying to catch up with his calm.

"Anything. Just tell me what's going on."

He hesitated. Then: "I need you to lie for me."

That landed hard.

"Lie?"

"Yes."

A beat.

"Michael... what's going on?"

"There's trouble coming. Maybe legal. Maybe worse. I'm in the middle of something, and I don't have time to explain."

"Is this about the firm?" she asked, voice tightening. The clients you didn't want to talk about?"

He didn't answer.

"Michael. What are you involved in?"

He exhaled steadily. "Something I should've walked away from a long time ago."

Her silence was answer enough.

I need time and distance. Andi, in about a week, I want you to start doing what everyone else is doing: put up flyers, call the precinct, and tell them you haven't heard from me since the morning of the attack. Tell them I worked in Tower One.

"You did work in Tower One."

"Exactly," he said. "Let them believe I died in it."

A beat. Then her voice, quiet: "You want me to report you missing."

"Yes."

"You want me to pretend my brother was crushed under a hundred floors of steel and glass."

"I know how it sounds."

"No, you don't. Because I've been living with grief since Tuesday. And now you want me to fake it for the world?"

He let the silence hang.

"Andrea... I'm not ready to come out of the shadows. I need this. I need space to think, to figure out what comes next. If I show my face now, it's over. For good."

More silence. Then she spoke, raw and real, "I hate this."

"I know."

"But I'll do it."

He closed his eyes, the pay phone's sticky receiver pressed tight to his ear.

"Thank you," he said. "I'll contact you soon. We'll figure out a secure way to communicate—no more phones."

"Michael... just promise me you're not going to vanish for good. Please."

"I'm not. I swear."

"I love you," she said.

"I love you too, sis."

He hung up. The line went dead with a soft click that echoed in the filthy lobby.

Manetti stayed for a moment longer, listening to the silence. Then he turned, stepped into the shadows of Bayou Street, and continued walking.

He had no idea where the path led. Only that he wasn't going back.Not yet.

CHAPTER 15

SOUTHBOUND

THE New Orleans Union Passenger Terminal smelled of disinfectants and diesel fuel.

Uniformed National Guardsmen stood under signs marked **Amtrak** and **Greyhound**, scanning bags and faces. Their rifles slung low. Their eyes higher.

The week after the Towers fell, America was on edge. Nobody said it out loud, but anyone who looked foreign, had a darker skin tone, or was off-script was pulled aside and searched. Manetti had the wrong kind of haircut for a bus station — too clean, too sharp. But his face wasn't foreign, and that helped.

He was wearing jeans now, Nikes, and a faded Saints T-shirt from a thrift store on Magazine Street. His lawyer's suit and tasseled shoes were tossed into a trash can on Canal Street.

He stood in line. He didn't speak.

When they stopped him, the Guard held out his hand. "ID."

Manetti gave him the Louisiana driver's license.

E. Dean Broussard

Born 1968.

New Orleans address.

The soldier flipped through a paper list. Checked again. Looked at the photo, then at Manetti.

"Where you headed?"

"Miami. Vacation."

"Got family down there?"

"No. Vacation."

The soldier held the passport for another beat, then handed it back.

"You're good."

Manetti exhaled.

******

The bus was clean. Cold air blew from the ceiling vents. Rows were half-empty. Most passengers were already asleep or trying to sleep.

He took a seat near the back, next to the window.

The wheels rolled out of the terminal. The Crescent City shrank behind them.

Through Mississippi and the panhandle of Florida, the view was pine trees, gas stations, and sun-bleached billboards.

The I-10 miles clicked behind. Biloxi. Pensacola. Tallahassee. Jacksonville.

At each stop, people shuffled off to smoke, eat, stretch, or disappear.

Manetti stayed in his seat at most stops.

He thought about the last time he flew to Miami—private jet, Gulfstream, firm business, champagne at the Breakers. This time, he was on a bus, drinking lukewarm coffee from a paper cup.

He smiled at the irony. It didn't feel like punishment. Not yet.

It felt like distance.

And distance was what he needed.

******

In Miami, he changed buses. Another Greyhound. Smaller. Older. More worn.

This one headed south. Past Homestead, down the spine of the Keys.

The Overseas Highway unspooled like a ribbon across the ocean.

Bridge after bridge. Key after key.

To the left: the Atlantic, blue and wild.

To the right: the Gulf, warm and flat.

In between: sailboats, wave runners, small fishing skiffs hugging the pilings.

Fishermen stood barefoot on narrow concrete walkways, casting lines into the water. Children with buckets of shrimp bait, and tourists squinting through sunglasses.

The sea went on forever in both directions.

He looked around the bus.

Budget tourists. College students. Drifters with nowhere left to go. The type of people who blend into the crowd.

That used to bother him.

Now, it made him feel safe.

As the bus rolled closer to Key West, Manetti rested his head against the window and stared out at the endless blue.

He still didn't have a plan.

But he had time.

And he had a name.

E. Dean Broussard.

Dead in the ground at Lafayette Cemetery.

But somehow, still breathing.

CHAPTER 16

MILE MARKER ZERO

The highway stretched like a thread through the sea and heat.

Thirty-four islands. Forty-two bridges. A strip of blacktop floating above turquoise water.

The final stretch of the trip. Four hours from Miami to Key West, with local stops along the way. Passing by mangroves and pastel-colored motels. Then, bait shops and sun-bleached bars with names like Hog Heaven and The Rum Line. Moving past old trestle bridges that once carried trains, now just rusted steel platforms used by local fishermen.

It felt like the end of something.

It was.

Key West wasn't just a place. It was an idea, a state of mind. A blur at the southern edge of the country, where people ran out of road and started over.

Barely four square miles across. Five feet above sea level. Closer to Havana than Miami. A city of bars, bones, and broken dreams.

The Spanish called it Cayo Hueso—Island of Bones. The limestone gleamed white under the sun, a graveyard turned postcard.

Now they call it Key West.

The Conchs called it home.

For Mike Manetti—now E. Dean Broussard—it was a hiding place. A map with no return address.

He knew the stories.

Hemingway wrote here. Soldiers and sailors retired here. Runaways, drunks, dreamers, grifters. Nobody asked too many questions—not if you paid your rent on time and didn't throw up in the wrong bar.

Tourists arrived on cruise ships and Harleys. They came for the sunsets, frozen drinks, and the feeling that nothing beyond the horizon mattered. To experience Margaritaville.

Manetti came for one reason.

To vanish.

******

The road ended at Mile Marker 0, where U.S. Route 1 simply… stopped. He stepped off the bus with a canvas duffel slung over one shoulder. Same clothes from the last leg. Same forged ID in his pocket. Same name in his head.

E. Dean Broussard.

New Orleans born. New life begun.

The heat hit him like a damp blanket. The salt in the air caught at his breath. Chickens wandered the streets. Scooters whined by. A drag queen waved from a bar porch with a cigar in her teeth.

This place was strange.

It was perfect.

He walked down Duval Street and looked like half the others — unsure, alone.

The kind of man who might have come here for a divorce. Or to dry out. Or to forget something important.

He found a room off Caroline Street, The Wharf Motel. Rented by the week. Cash up front. No questions asked.

He sat on the edge of the bed, opened the window, relaxed for the first time in days, and listened to the wind move through the palms.

He was at the end of the highway.

And, maybe, the beginning of something else.

A week later a name appeared at the bottom of the *New York Post*'s third page spread. Small font. Just another in the sea of the gone.

Michael Manetti, 33. Attorney at Simon & Kershaw. Last seen the morning of September 11, presumed to have been in his office during the attacks. Reported missing by his sister, Andrea Manetti of Manhattan.

No further details.

Only silence.

CHAPTER 17

THE GIRL AT THE END OF THE WORLD

THE Wharf Motel was decent enough. No extras. Salt air seeped through the window seams, and the bedsheets faintly smelled of salt and ocean.

Manetti showered, shaved, and changed into a clean polo, creased jeans, and Nikes. Blended in just enough.

The desk clerk recommended a local diner off White Street. Grilled grouper, good coffee. He ate quietly, watching the regulars come and go. Nobody paid him any mind. That was good.

After dinner, he walked west along Front Street. Charter boats tugged at their ropes in the slips at the Key West Bight. Nets drying. Bait buckets stacked. The night air was thick with salt, humidity, and freshly caught fish.

He stepped into a bar called The Fisherman's Net. Low ceiling, plank floor, dartboard beyond the pool table. It smelled like beer, bait, and tobacco. Men in T-shirts and sun-bleached baseball caps shouted over each another at the bar. Someone had a harmonica. It was that kind of place.

He took a seat at the bar. Ordered a beer. Kept to himself.

At the dartboard, a crew was laughing loudly. Mostly men. One woman. She stood out.

She moved as if she belonged there. Long legs, tan body, sun-steaked brown hair tied into a ponytail. The broad shoulders hinted swimmer. Her stance was confident among the men. When she smiled, the room seemed to tilted a little.

She caught his eye. Smiled again.

The game died down. The men peeled off. She picked up her beer and walked straight to him.

"What brings you to Key West, Eli?" she said.

Stunned by the name. Coincidence? Manetti's hand paused on his glass. The answer would have to wait.

He turned, calm, and smiled. "Eli? That the name for strangers down here?"

She grinned. "No. It's your Ivy League uniform. The 'Elis' of Yale, get it."

"Guilty," he said. "Guess I missed the part about the Key West dress code."

"You pressed a crease in those jeans, didn't you?" Emily scoffs.

He looked down. Shrugged. "Old habit."

She leaned against the bar. Closer now.

"Your mates?" he asked, gesturing with his chin toward the dartboard.

"Yeah. They work the boats. One of them's my ex. Ex-boyfriend that is."

Manetti pulled an empty barstool over. "Have a seat. Can I buy you another?", motioning toward her near-empty bottle. She took the seat, left her empty bottle on the bar.

"You work the boats too?" Manetti asked.

"Sometimes. I help my father part-time, keeping the books, taking reservations, and making coffee. I step on the *Kitty Jo*, my father's boat, when Kenny—he's the ex—can't stand upright."

"Kenny sounds reliable."

"He's got a good heart. Just didn't want to leave this place. I tried. College, some big dreams. But after my dad's heart scare… I came back. Started to love it here."

"My real job is at R.E.E.F.S., where I organize rallies and community awareness".

She finished her beer.

"What's R.E.E.F.S?"

"A grassroots environmental protection group. Responsible Environmental Efforts for the Florida Straits."

"Some people chase more. I learned to be happy with less," as she rested her back against the bar.

"You're a romantic," Manetti said.

"No. Just not blind."

They talked for another hour. Beer. Small stories. Big silences in between.

She was different from the women he knew in New York. No pretense, no polish. She wore authenticity like sunscreen—applied thick, without apology.

He liked that.

"Getting hungry?" she asked with a suggestion in mind.

"Since you're new in town, apparently alone, and single… you don't have a wife back at a resort hotel, do you?" she rhetorically asked, glancing at his bare ring finger. "And since I'm a good Conch citizen, I feel obligated to invite a stranger to dinner. Me and my father, Captain Jim. No pressure. But you'll eat better than diner food."

"You just met me. What if I'm dangerous?"

She laughed. "You wear pressed jeans. You're not dangerous."

"Fair point."

He stood. Extended a hand.

"Dean Broussard," he said.

"Emily Foster," she replied. "Pleased to meet you, *Eli*."

They both laughed. Then walked out together into the warm night air.

CHAPTER 18

DINNER WITH THE CAPTAIN

THE Foster cottage sat two blocks from the water, with a narrow porch and shuttered windows. Its paint was worn soft from the salt air. When they stepped inside, the screen door creaked then clapped shut, a sound that reminded Manetti of his family's Bronx walkup with the summer screen door.

Inside, it smelled like old wood and food on the stove. A ceiling fan ticked overhead, slow and steady.

"Hi, Dad. I brought a friend," Emily called out.

From the kitchen: "Hope your friend's hungry. Yellowtail's almost done."

Jim Foster appeared, a dishtowel over his shoulder. Sixty-something. Navy build, steady in his stance. Tanned, like a man who's spent time at sea. He saw Manetti and smiled.

"Well, unfamiliar face. Name's Jim," extending a hand.

"Dean Broussard," Manetti said, offering his hand. "Emily was kind enough to take pity on a stranger."

Jim shook it. Firm. "Strangers are just friends we haven't fed yet."

Emily laughed and kissed her father on the cheek. "Dean can help me set the table."

The living room was small, cool, and filled with quiet history. Framed photos of ships and sailors. A black-and-white of a young Jim Foster in Navy dress blues, with his arm around a laughing woman—likely Emily's mother. There were also pictures of Emily, including swim meets, a graduation cap, ribbons, and swimming trophies hanging along the bookshelf, all fading memories.

There were books on marine biology, weather patterns, and reef health. The kind of volumes kept by someone who is always learning and stays curious.

A fishnet hung from the ceiling beam above the couch. A faded conch shell rested beside a cigar box marked "TACKLE."

Emily brought out plates and napkins. Jim called from the kitchen: "Dinner's served."

They sat around the table beneath a dim pendant light. Manetti caught the aroma of butter, garlic, citrus, and something fried. He was hungrier than he had realized.

"Yellowtail snapper, pan-seared," Jim announced. "And conch fritters, for that real Key West tang."

"They smell amazing," Manetti said. "Better than anything I've had in a long time."

Emily poured iced tea. "Or beer?" she asked.

"Beer's good."

They ate. The food was simple and perfect. The snapper fell apart on the fork. The fritters were crispy on the outside, soft and peppery inside.

"So," Jim said, "what brings you to the end of the road?"

Manetti swallowed. Thought fast.

"I was in Miami last week. I had a vacation planned. Then the towers came down. I work uptown, in Manhattan. I read some friends downtown didn't make it. I needed... air."

Jim nodded. "Terrible thing. I served twenty-two years. Never thought we'd see a strike like that on home soil."

Emily looked at Manetti sympathetically and said, "I'm sorry."

"Thanks. I don't know how long I'll stay. Just taking some time before I go back."

"What do you do?"

"Lawyer. For a bank." He let that hang, vague enough to move on.

Jim didn't press. "Well, you picked a good place to disappear for a bit.", he said prophetically.

As the food disappeared, so did the barriers. The conversation shifted to local topics—weather, storms, fishing conditions, and how the tourists were ruining everything.

"Not all sunsets and rum drinks," Jim said. "Storms come hard down here. You've got to make your own calm."

Emily added, "We live close to nature here. Hurricanes, reef die-off, coral bleaching, and overfishing are all part of it. I used to think I'd leave after college. But I stayed. It grows on you."

"She's got a degree in marine biology," Jim said, fatherly pride in his voice. "Could've gone anywhere. Stayed to help her old man run a boat."

Emily shrugged. "Sometimes life isn't about more. It's about *enough*."

After dinner, Jim brought out a photo album. He showed them

a shot of the *Kitty Jo*—his charter boat named after Emily's mother, Katherine Josephine.

"She passed a few years ago," Jim said. "The boat keeps her close."

They talked for another hour. Manetti listened more than he spoke. Careful. Controlled. But part of him wasn't pretending anymore.

The food, the home, the warmth—it all felt real.

He hadn't felt real in a while.

At the door, Emily walked him out to the porch.

"Thanks for inviting me. Your dad's a great cook. The conch fritters reminded me of Rhode Island clam cakes."

Emily smiled. "Same salt, different shore."

They stood close now. The Key West breeze warm off the Gulf.

"Nice to meet you, Dean. Maybe we'll see you around town before you leave."

"I hope so," Manetti said. And meant it.

"Fins Up!" she said with a smile, as they said goodnight.

CHAPTER 19

THE WALK HOME

The night was warm.

Not hot. Not heavy. Just warm enough to feel the cool sea breeze touch your skin.

Manetti walked alone back through the dark streets of Old Town. Past closed shops. Past flickering porch lights. Past drunken laughter and the crack of pool balls spilling out of bars.

The sidewalk was uneven, cracked in places where banyan roots pushed up from below. He walked slowly, head down, hands in his pockets.

He wasn't thinking about the FBI. Not about the firm. Not even about Patrilla.

He was thinking about Emily.

And what she said.

"Some people chase more. I learned to be happy with less."

He used to chase everything.

Money. Prestige. Apartments with high ceilings and park views. Women dressed in pearls for dinner and drinking martinis for effect.

He had the watch. The car service. The Lexington Avenue

address.

But none of it lasted. Not the money. Not the women. Not even the name.

He was a ghost now. Not even thirty-five. Already a shadow.

He had plenty of money hidden in foreign banks and ownership in his co-op. But now, he was hiding in a motel room with a false passport. A name borrowed from a dead boy in a New Orleans cemetery. Is that what his life had come to? he wondered.

He turned the corner past a hedge of hibiscus and paused at a low stone wall. Sat for a while.

The moon was high over the water. Palm fronds rustled somewhere behind him.

He thought of what Emily said over dinner.

"It's not about more. It's about enough."

Emily's words kept turning in his head. Would there ever be an *enough* for him?

He'd skimmed gold filings as a kid, thinking it was clever. Laundered millions for men who would kill to keep what they had. He dressed it up as business—a game. A way to outsmart the rules. Victimless crimes.

But what did it buy?

Not safety. Not peace. Not love.

He'd always thought money meant freedom.

But the men who paid him were caught up in it. Paranoid. Always scheming, always watching. Most would not die in peace.

And now he was on the run himself. From the life he had built. From the ghosts he helped create.

All that money. All that cleverness.

It hadn't bought him anything that mattered.

He thought of Emily again.

The easy way she moved.

The way she talked about the sea, about her father, about her little island world with no pretense.

She knew who she was.

He didn't.

Not anymore.

******

The wind shifted and carried the scent of salt and bougainvillea. He stood, brushed sand off the seat of his pants, and kept walking.

The streets narrowed. The porch lights dimmed.

At the end of the lane, the Wharf Motel sat in darkness. Room 6. Thin sheets, a ceiling fan ticking like a tired metronome.

But for the first time in a long while, Manetti wasn't planning anything.

He wasn't calculating.

He was just thinking.

And for now, that was enough.

CHAPTER 20

THE HORROR HITS HOME

The headlines didn't let up.

EVERY day—more names, more photos. Smiling faces taped to chain-link fences, bus stops, and the plywood walls near Ground Zero. "Have you seen…?" scrawled in black marker. Desperate handwriting. Weathered and faded fliers. Burnt-out candles beneath them.

But nobody was coming home.

Manetti sat alone on the only chair in his motel room. The fan blew hot air across the room. On the nightstand: cold coffee, a Styrofoam container with half a fried grouper sandwich, and a folded copy of *USA Today*.

The weekend edition.

He flipped through it carefully, hesitantly, as if moving slowly might alter the truth.

The names were in alphabetical order. The photos were small. Faces frozen in time.

He saw Sally Hastings' name first.

No story. Just her age, name, hometown, and the photo she'd

used on her work ID badge. A faint smile, as if she was about to say something clever.

He read the name three times. Still didn't feel real.

Then, a half page down, Jane Sampson, his administrative assistant.

He had known Jane for three years. She managed his schedule, proofread his filings, and guarded his office like a fortress. She was sharp, loyal, and never nosy but always aware.

Gone.

And Sally.

He hadn't called it love. Not yet. Maybe not ever. But there was something there. A slow burn. The way she looked at him when she thought he wasn't watching. The weekend in Spring Lake. How she asked him questions no one else did. The kind of questions that demanded honesty.

She was funny. And bold. And younger than she should've been to die.

Manetti leaned back against the headboard, eyes shut. The image of her smile played behind his lids.

It had only been a few weeks. But it felt much longer.

Years.

He thought about Sally's family and what they must be going through. The phone that will never ring. Her empty teenage bed. The voicemail they still listen to at night, just to hear her voice.

They wouldn't know much or anything about him. She hadn't talked much about her parents. Maybe she hadn't told them. Maybe he didn't matter.

He couldn't call the Hastings. He couldn't write or publicly mourn her. He couldn't even say her name aloud without risking everything.

More names appeared. More dead from the firm.

Partners. Associates. Mailroom kids. Clients in for early meetings.

He scanned each page like a survivor reading a ship's log, waiting to see who else had gone under.

The newspaper said that bodies were still being pulled from the rubble. Still reporting tons of twisted steel and ash being trucked out to Staten Island. They were sifting through it all—bone fragments, wallet photos, clothing, shoes.

Some names would never be matched.

Over eleven hundred people with no identifiable remains.

It hit him, then. Like a slow knife.

He should've been there.

He *was* there.

And he walked out.

Jane didn't. Sally didn't. The two F.B.I. special agents, Turci and Alves, who were there only to see him because of his crimes, didn't. None of them made it.

But he did.

By inches. By seconds. By a goddamned stairway, a broken window, and a twist of luck.

And now he was hiding in Key West under the name of a dead boy, reading the obituary of a woman who once held his hand on the boardwalk… held him close in bed.

The air in the room grew thick. The fan clacked louder. The walls leaned in close.

He got up. Threw the paper in the trash. Didn't finish the sandwich.

He turned out the light and lay in the dark.

And for the first time since the towers fell, he cried.

No sound. Quiet sniffling.

A few tears slid down his cheek as he stared at the ceiling, listening to the fan and remembering Sally's laugh.

And wondering if her memory and the emotions brought to the surface might save him.

Thinking of Sally's family and their loss, he thought of his sister.

It was time to call Andrea... one last time.

Andrea stuck to the plan.

The one they'd whispered across a payphone line nearly three weeks earlier.

She filed the report like the others had. Posted flyers near Union Square, the Upper East Side, and down by the churches near Canal Street.

Black-and-white copies.
Stapled with hope.

She told the NYPD the same story everyone else was telling. That her brother was missing. That she hadn't heard from him since the morning of the attacks.

Maybe he lost his phone. Maybe he was injured. Maybe, just maybe, he was alive somewhere, trying to get home.

She cried when she said it. Not an act, but honest grief. Dead or alive, she feared never seeing him again.

She didn't tell them he had called.

She didn't tell anyone.

That was the plan.

Hold the line.

Let the world think he vanished.

Until the rest could be figured out.

******

There was a pay-as-you-go internet café on Caroline Street, two blocks from the Wharf Motel. Manetti had used it once before—for coffee, for quiet and solace. Now he needed it for something else.

He slid into a seat by the back wall, inserted coins into the terminal, and waited for the screen to load. The keyboard was sticky, and the air was thick with fresh espresso.

He opened a browser window and created a burner email address at *open.com*.

User name: *lazarus1*

Password: *TheBronx*

Short. Unforgettable. Biblical, in its way. Then typed a message.

"Love you, sis."

Saved as draft and logged out.

Then he stepped outside, fed a few quarters into the payphone bolted to the alley wall. The receiver clicked. A faint dial tone followed. He dialed.

Andrea picked up on the second ring.

"Michael?" Her voice cracked. "Are you okay? Where are you?"

"I'm okay," he said. "But I can't say where. I need you to listen carefully—this may be the last time we talk like this for a while."

"Why? Why can't we just—?"

"Because if anyone starts looking, they'll pull phone records. Maybe tap lines. I don't want them using you to find me. We need to switch to digital dead drops. Safer this way."

She paused. Then: "Okay. Tell me what to do."

"Go to an internet café or library. Anywhere public. Do not use your home computer. Got it?"

"Got it."

"I created an email account on *Open.com* with the login name lazarus1. The password is TheBronx, capital T, capital B. Memorize it. Then destroy whatever you wrote it on."

She was quiet again. Writing, probably.

"Here's how we use it. You log in, write me a message, and save it as a draft. *Never send it.* Just save as a draft, I'll do the same. I'll check it early every week. You can check it at the end of each week."

"No sent messages. No replies. Just the draft box.", Andrea repeated.

"Exactly. I'll delete each one after I read it."

"What if I need to reach you fast?"

"You won't. Not yet. I just created a message for you. Read it and leave a message as a draft. Then we'll know it works."

"I understand," she said. "Michael… are you safe?"

There was a long pause.

"I'm alive," he said. "That's what matters now."

Later that day, Andrea walked to the small public library near 86th Street. She logged into the account from a basement terminal, read his message, and left a draft.

Are you really okay?

Three days later, the message was gone.

Replaced by one line: *Still standing. Keep the faith.*

A secret phrase between them from CYO camp to "stay vigilant."

CHAPTER 21

SIGHTING

October 22, 2001

FRANKIE Dellaro sat in a diner off the Palisades Parkway, spooning sugar into his coffee when he found it. Third column, page B3 of a two-week-old New York Herald-Courier. Coffee-stained, with pages yellowing and folded between puzzles and sports.

Headline:

"North Tower Survivor Recalls Escape, Offers New Detail"

Byline:

Avery Dandridge, Staff Reporter

October 8, 2001

In the weeks following the attacks on the World Trade Center, stories of survival continue to emerge.

Michael Gormley, 47, a partner with Manhattan-based accounting firm Allen and Cress, recounted his narrow escape from the South Tower on the morning of September 11.

"I was on the 76th floor copy room when we felt the jolt," Gormley said. "We didn't know what had happened. Lights flickered, the copier

stopped, then rebooted. Phones weren't working. Someone said we were ordered to evacuate the building. Elevators weren't stopping, so we started down the stairwell."

Gormley, who fractured two ribs in the descent, said one moment stood out vividly. "When I reached the lobby, I'm sure I saw Manetti—Mike Manetti—I knew him from the law firm Simon & Kershaw. He was standing near an opening in the glass doors. He was helping a woman who'd fallen. He had blood on his shirt. I didn't stop. People were pushing forward. It was dark with dust, but I remember his face. We passed each other earlier that morning on the Concourse escalator. Little doubt in my mind, it was him."

When asked why that memory mattered, Gormley's voice faltered.

"Because Manetti's name is on the missing list. He's presumed dead. But I'm sure I saw him. He was alive in the lobby. I figured he made it. I just assumed... until I saw his name."

Gormley never saw him again.

Manetti, a senior financial attorney at Simon & Kershaw, was listed among the presumed deceased in a memorial published by the firm on September 19.

"It doesn't make sense," Gormley added. "But a lot of that day doesn't."

Frankie read it twice. Then again.

Then he lit a cigarette with shaking fingers and called Sonny Patrilla.

CHAPTER 22

THE INTRUDER

THE lock was old brass, tarnished by years of handling. The intruder didn't need a key.

He waited until dusk, hidden in the shadow of the recessed doorway at the bodega across the street. Andrea Manetti's building stood like so many on the Upper West Side: brick, fifteen stories, with decorative cornices worn by time. He easily found the apartment number. Her name, *A. Manetti*, was on the buzzer panel. He had watched her come and go for three days, always alone.

A tenant let him in without thinking, distracted by a phone call and two small dogs pulling at leashes.

He took the stairs. Quietly. Always the stairs.

Apartment 3 B.

He listened for a moment. Silence. Then he slipped a rake pick and tension wrench into the lock, manipulated the cylinders, and turned them. One click. Then another. The door gently open.

Inside, it was dark except for the soft ambient glow of the city filtering through gauzy curtains. The space smelled like lavender. Tidy. Efficient. Lived-in by someone who liked control but didn't always have time to maintain it.

A wine rack sat next to a wall-mounted bookshelf. Half-read novels leaned against medical journals, folders labeled *Legal Services NYC*, and a yoga mat still rolled up by the door. She left a teacup in the sink and a silk scarf over the back of a low-slung couch. A small pair of running shoes were tucked neatly near the radiator.

Professional. Single. No pets. No man's shoes.

He moved through the apartment with gloved fingers.

Desk drawers opened and closed. Her laptop was password-protected, but the mail tray wasn't—mostly junk, flyers, a thick envelope from the Office of the Chief Medical Examiner, and another from a New York grief counseling service.

He took note, kept moving.

The bedroom featured a wall of built-in cabinets, with clothes arranged by color and season. Photos pinned to a linen corkboard above the dresser displayed snapshots of happier times—Andrea and her brother Mike at the beach as children, a high school graduation, her in a cap and gown, and one older photo that stopped him cold.

It showed two men and a boy in front of a tattoo salon storefront—the boy was clearly Mike Manetti, no older than twelve. Scribbled in a feminine hand on the back were the words: Dad, Sailor, and Mike. New Orleans '79. Another photo showed the dark curly hair and snarly smile of a kid likely headed for juvie. A third was a framed photograph of three smiling soldiers in jungle camo, one pointing to a crude tattoo on his arm. On the back, someone had written, Sailor gave Tommy the ink. Vietnam 1967.

"Sailor. Tattoos. New Orleans," the intruder muttered to himself.

Satisfied, he returned the photos to their places. He didn't take them. Didn't need to. His memory was good, and he had something to start his search.

But as he turned toward the door, he pulled out a short brown cigarette, lit it, and took a couple of long drags. He exhaled the last puff near the cracked-open kitchen window, thinking the breeze would carry the smoke out.

It didn't.

The faint scent lingered.

The intruder crushed the butt and flushed it. He looked around again. No mess. No drawers left open. No lights on. He wiped the doorknob and slipped back into the hallway.

By the time Andrea Manetti walked back in from her Pilates class, her apartment would feel just as it always had—safe, personal, untouched.

Except for one thing.

As she hung her keys on the hook and kicked off her athletic shoes, she paused in the doorway.

There it was. A faint scent.

Cigarette smoke.

Fresh. Not hers.

She blinked. Sniffed again. Could have been the hallway… the neighbor.

She didn't smoke. None of her friends did. Something about it didn't sit right.

She glanced around the room. Everything appeared in place.

She poured a glass of wine, but the feeling— that flicker of uneasiness—didn't fade.

Not that night. Not for days.

CHAPTER 23

BLOOD AND INK

T HE morning air was already thick, a blanket of humidity clinging
to the palm fronds above the Wharf Motel.

Manetti stepped outside into the courtyard. A gravel crunch
underfoot marked the narrow path to the office; a low, sun-faded
building with a stucco exterior stained by mildew. An old man on
a bicycle rode by with a plastic milk crate strapped to the rear,
humming something slow and off-key. Across the street, two Cuban
men argued in Spanish over a domino game set up on a paint-peeled
picnic table.

Bougainvillea spilled over chain-link fences. A pair of lizards
chased each other beneath the battered Coca-Cola machine outside
the office. The clerk, a gaunt retiree with nicotine-stained fingers
and a perpetual squint, barely looked up as Manetti passed by with
his coffee.

The motel's tiny courtyard had three plastic chairs and a
weathered umbrella staked into a patch of gravel. A pile of yesterday's
newspapers sat on a chipped metal table near the vending machines.

Manetti sifted through them, paused at the headline in the *USA*

Today regional news section. He nearly dropped his cup.

Noted Tattoo Artist Murdered

NEW ORLEANS, La. — A brutal attack left Dominic "Sailor" DeJesus, a well-known local tattoo artist, dead Thursday afternoon in a Water Street rooming house. DeJesus, 56, was transported to Good Shepherd Hospital by ambulance and later died of cardiac arrest, which doctors attributed to injuries sustained in a beating.

Authorities say the victim was discovered by a neighbor who grew concerned after not seeing DeJesus for two days. The assailant remains unknown.

"He was a tough guy with a soft side," said a tenant who asked not to be identified. "We all called him Sailor. Never caused trouble. Just cared for his snakes and drank his beer."

A decorated Army veteran, DeJesus served with the 173rd Airborne Brigade and was present at the 1967 Battle of Đắk Tô. He had no known next of kin.

Witnesses provided conflicting descriptions of a male suspect seen entering the building. Police have released no further details and are asking for the public's help.

Manetti sat still. His breath was shallow. A sick heat bloomed in his chest.

He'd known this was possible—inevitable, maybe. But seeing Sailor's name in print, under *murdered,* was something else.

He read it again. The descriptions were vague. No arrest. No real leads.

Which made it worse.

Someone had gone looking. Someone asking questions. Someone who needed names—and direction.

Sailor didn't have a reason to lie to a man holding a knife or gun.

Manetti lowered the paper slowly.

That's how it ends for Sailor, he thought. In a single column. No war medals. No tribute. Just another man with a past who finally couldn't outrun it.

He stared across the courtyard. A dragonfly hovered in place, wings slicing through the air. A lawnmower hummed softly two blocks away. He felt it now—tightness in his chest. That familiar feeling from the Bronx. When your gut warns you that it's not just bad luck.

Back in his room, Manetti locked the door and pulled the curtain tight. He sat on the bed, rereading the article, each word feeling heavier than the last.

Did they get what they wanted? he wondered.

Manetti stood abruptly, crossed the room, checked the mirror. His eyes looked different now. Harder.

The Patrilla family. They had reason. And now, maybe, they were cleaning house.

The murder of Sailor indicated someone was tying up loose ends. Someone worried that the man presumed dead might actually be alive—and very dangerous.

And that someone, he realized, was leaving bodies.

He could imagine Sonny's voice: "If he's dead, fine. If he ain't— make him."

CHAPTER 24

CLAIMS AND CONSEQUENCES

December 2000

THE Claims Inquiry Office of Trinity Life and Casualty Company was located three subway stops and a five-block walk from the Brooklyn Bridge, on the second floor of a faded brick commercial building that once housed an early-century printing company. Unlike the glass towers in Midtown, where Trinity's corporate leaders worked behind ergonomic desks with panoramic views, the Brooklyn office had gathered decades of dust and silence. The carpet was a worn gray. The office furniture, chipped and heavy, had the bleak charm and enduring presence of a morgue.

It had a faint smell of musty paper and old radiator heat. The fluorescent lights hummed, providing a steady background to the clicking of keyboards.

Cal Winters presided over the department from a raised platform like a retired sea captain on a weathered bridge. His desk overlooked three clerks and two investigator desks. One of those desks remained unclaimed until now, serving as a reminder of Jim Cahill's recent retirement. A Pinkerton man through and through,

Cahill handled Trinity's strangest claims for thirty years and left the company with his final case closed—and a fraud trial pending.

The new man occupying Cahill's old leather swivel chair was Rocco "Rocky" Rossi.

Rossi's first day had been quiet. He hung his old olive trench coat on the rack by the door, dropped his MetroCard into a drawer, and sat as if he had been coming there for years. At fifty-five, with a busted nose and hands like meat hooks, Rossi radiated the air of a man who didn't bluff. He'd been a homicide detective in Trenton before a tangle with the DA's office over search procedures that led him into early retirement. He left with full benefits and zero regrets. Justice meant more to him than office politics. Cal Winters liked that.

Rossi kept a photo of his daughter and grandson on his desk next to the computer monitor. The kid was special to him because his rat of a father abandoned the family. Rossi paid for his Catholic school tuition and looked after the boy and his mother.

He didn't talk much; he listened and took notes in pen. He carried a notebook the size of a cigarette pack, writing in block letters. He often read files while leaning back, with his left foot resting on the corner of his desk.

On the first day, Cal introduced him to the clerks—Joan, Lisa, and Ramona—then dropped a case folder on his desk.

"This is a real case, not a drill," Cal said. "Guy disappeared in Louisiana three years ago. Apparent boating accident. Boat found, but no body." The case was considered an accidental death. Under New Jersey state law, the beneficiary could petition the court for a declaration of desertion after seven years, before filing on the life insurance benefit.

"Funny thing, the guy's body turned up last year. I never liked the claim. Too clean." Winters said.

"Classic," Rossi muttered, flipping it open. "Let me guess. Wife's clean on paper. Finances were a mess."

Cal raised an eyebrow. "You've got it."

"I've seen it before. One time, the wife hired a hitman, but he fell in love with her, then she turned him in."

"I'll miss Jim, liked him," Cal said. "But I think you'll do. Look into it".

Rossi cracked a small grin. "I don't need to be liked. Just listened to."

Two years after his disappearance, the murdered man's body was found in a Savannah motel room.

The case followed a familiar pattern—debts pile up, man disappears, body is found pointing to homicide, widow claims her life insurance. When Rossi reviewed the file, what caught his attention was the contrast between the man's disappearance and the widow's actions. Her bank statements showed little grief since the settlement. Vacations. New furniture. A week at a Maine resort.

"She got lucky or stupid. If the husband were a missing person, she'd still be waiting four more years to start her claim. This way, she filed immediately to collect on the insurance." Rossi noted to Winters. "People get weird when they've been betrayed."

Three shots to the torso. Motel room. No sign of robbery. All identification intact.

The press called it tragic. The sheriff called it unsolved. The wife collected the life insurance benefit.

Rossi called it unfinished business and flew to Georgia to reopen the case, his first with Trinity.

He talked with the motel maid, the front desk clerk, and a waitress at the Waffle House two blocks away, who was waiting for a bus near the motel. They all remembered the case, which drew a lot of attention. The maid testified to seeing the man and woman arguing near the ice machine on the night of the murder. Somehow, the police never interviewed her. Later, her testimony proved to be consistent.

Back in Brooklyn, Rossi subpoenaed the widow's bank account and credit card statements, revealing her flight to Savannah around the time the body was discovered. Turns out the husband owned an unregistered SIG Sauer 9mm P320 handgun. Rossi presented his findings to the Savannah P.D. and the Chatham County D.A. A search warrant was issued for the gun. Ballistics matched up. Confronted with the new evidence and being identified as the woman arguing at the motel, she confessed to killing her S.O.B. husband and took a plea.

The widow had found him, then finished the job.

Trinity recovered the benefit from her remaining assets. The D.A. added insurance fraud to the murder one indictment.

The case never made the *Times*, but it landed in the *Brooklyn Eagle*, a page three column with Rossi's name omitted at his request.

He wasn't in it for credit. He was in it for the truth.

******

A year later, in December 2001, Rossi was reviewing claim files when a new folder appeared on his desk. The header read: Beneficiary Inquiry – on the life of Michael Manetti.

It was flagged for a routine internal review. Standard life policy. Insured: Michael J. Manetti. Presumed dead in the World Trade Center collapse. Beneficiary: Andrea Manetti, sister.

The date of death was September 11, 2001.

Due to the exceptional circumstances, statutes were amended to permit the beneficiaries of 9/11 victims to file life insurance claims without the usual seven-year waiting period—an unusual waiver of red tape.

Trinity insured the lives of several Simon & Kershaw executives through a group life plan. 9/11 claims had been filed and routinely cleared quickly. This one felt different.

Rossi raised an eyebrow at the familiar name.

The name was linked to a federal racketeering investigation into the Patrilla crime family. Rossi was informally aware of it through quiet conversations with FBI colleagues. Two Special Agents assigned to the case were killed when the towers collapsed. The investigation stalled after the terror attacks.

He tapped the folder against his desk. Then opened it.

This time, it wasn't just about insurance fraud.

It could be about something bigger.

CHAPTER 25

CLAIMS AND SHADOWS

THE late fall sun cast long shadows across the Upper West Side. A few remaining orange and crimson leaves clung stubbornly to tree branches lining West End Avenue, while gusts swept dry scraps of newspaper and candy wrappers along the curbs. The building, its stonework softened by decades of wind and soot, the front lobby a dim wash of yellow light behind old glass doors.

At exactly 6:02 p.m., Rocco "Rocky" Rossi pressed the buzzer for Apartment 3 B.

"Yes?" Andrea's voice crackled faintly through the speaker.

"Miss Manetti? Rocco Rossi. Claims Inquiry with Trinity Life. Here for our appointment."

A brief pause. Then the door clicked open.

She met him at the elevator, her auburn hair pinned loosely, her expression a mixture of suspicion and polite restraint. "Good evening," she said.

"Good evening, ma'am." Rossi's tone was soft but clipped, well-worn from decades of witness interviews. "Thanks for making the time to see me."

"Yes, of course. Please come in."

Inside, the apartment showed signs of self-sufficiency: modest, clean, tasteful. The dark hardwood floor creaked softly under Rossi's weight. The foyer opened into a cozy living room with warm light and colors. The kitchen beyond was galley-style—white cabinets, Pottery Barn pans hanging from a wall rack. The aroma of freshly brewed coffee filled the air.

"Coffee?" she offered.

"Yeah. Black's fine, thank you."

When she entered the kitchen, Rossi gave the room a slow scan, his trained eye moving like radar across each object. It was the small, subtle details that mattered — personality or inconsistency. A small desk in the corner held a keyboard and monitor. The desktop was otherwise clean except for a mail bin and a notepaper holder. The wall behind the desk was a mosaic for a theater lover: signed black and yellow Playbills in floating frames, vintage play and movie posters, and a collection of family photos. The CPU tower on the floor and the broadband modem beside it made one thing clear: she had internet at home.

He sat on the edge of the couch and waited, his eyes briefly resting on a framed photo of a young man, probably her brother Michael Manetti, standing next to Andrea in Central Park.

Andrea returned with two steaming mugs. "Here you are."

Thanks. You must be a theater fan, he said as he gestured toward the wall. I'm not much myself, but my daughter is, and my grandson. He's ten, loves musicals. I don't know. I guess that's okay. She's been hinting that she'd like to see Mama Mia. Have you seen it yet?

As she took her seat, Andrea replied, "No, not yet. Tickets are still hard to get, and they're so expensive now. Not like when I was a kid and my mom would take me to the Saturday matinee for less than ten dollars."

"Yeah," Rossi said, "I'm saving up to take them into town for a show and dinner. They live in Trenton. They'll like that."

Rossi transitions with a sip of coffee.

"Mind if I ask a few routine questions for the file?"

She nodded, then carefully settled into the chair opposite him.

"You're listed as the sole beneficiary of your brother's policy, correct?"

"Yes. He never married. Our parents passed, so he named me." She spoke evenly, but her fingers fussed briefly with the coffee handle.

"You two close?"

A beat. "Yes, but we didn't see each other often. He worked long hours, very private. Typical high-powered attorney, I guess."

"Do you know if he has any other policies with other beneficiaries?"

"No. I can't imagine anyone else."

Rossi nodded. "Simon & Kershaw. Wall Street. Lotta sharks in that water. From what I understand, Michael was a rising star there. Did he ever talk about the kind of clients he handled?"

"Not really," she said... a little too fast.

Rossi let that hang in the air a moment. "Ever mention Anthony Patrilla?"

Andrea blinked. Her cup hovered mid-air. "I—I've read the name in the papers."

"Not what I asked."

"No," she said more firmly, "Michael never spoke of him. Why would he?"

"He's a very dangerous guy, that's all," Rossi offered.

Rossi shifted slightly in his seat, setting the mug down with a quiet clink. "Patrilla is on a DOJ watchlist. We know Simon & Kershaw did legal work for him. There's suspicion that your brother could have been involved in money laundering. Did you know anything about that?"

Andrea looked away. "I'm sorry. I don't know anything about that."

Her tone was clipped. Defensive.

Rossi tried to arouse any sign of grief.

"Have you made any arrangements for…" Rossi hesitated, "for a memorial service or the like, Miss Manetti? Not important to me, but I hear it can bring closure to some."

"No, everything has been so confusing, and we don't have family. I don't even know who his friends are. So, no plans at this time."

During the interview, Andrea showed no signs of grief when discussing her only family member. No sobs. No signs of sadness.

Could he rattle her with another question? he wondered.

"Last time you spoke to him?"

"What do you mean, Mr. Rossi? He died in the towers' collapse," Andrea said defensively.

"I'm sorry, I understand that. Just wondering when, before the attack, how frequently did you talk?"

Confused and suspicious about such questions, Andrea snapped back, "Mr. Rossi, he was my brother. We lived in different worlds. He was very busy with his career. We didn't talk regularly, if that's what you mean, but he would call now and then to check in and see how I was doing. I believe the last time we spoke was probably mid-August. But I don't see why that's important."

"No reason, ma'am, just want to close the timeline."

He paused, softened his voice.

"Miss Manetti, this is the part of the job no one likes. Asking family to re-live events. But it's standard. Fraud's rare, but it happens. We just like the files to match up cleanly."

"Fraud?" She responds, her lips tightened.

"My company insured the lives of several senior-level employees and partners of Simon & Kershaw. Most have not yet filed claims. You filed earlier than most. Do you have financial stress that could be alleviated by the settlement?"

"Mr. Rossi, you are upsetting me with these questions. I think you should leave. I was advised to submit the claim. It was not my idea. I don't need the money. Unless you have more pertinent questions, please leave," Andrea orders.

"No more questions, I think we're good." He rose, his tone easy. "Again, my condolences. I'll see myself out."

Rossi exited with the casual gait of someone who'd just wrapped a routine task. But he didn't leave the block.

From a half block away, across West End Avenue, he watched and waited.

His instincts were spot on. Within thirty minutes, Andrea exited her building. Headed south.

He followed at a distance, trailing her through the early evening foot traffic. It might be just an errand, but experience told him that when suspects get rattled, they can act impulsively. As she turned onto Broadway, her pace quickened. Rossi stayed safely back. Andrea turned into a storefront below the neon sign Bytes & Beans Internet Café, glowing orange through the misty dark. Through the plate glass window with colorful posters advertising local events and notices of missing cats and dogs, he watched her take terminal #3. Her back to the window.

He saw the computer in her apartment and the internet modem. Why, other than to hide her activity, would she use a public terminal, he wondered. She wasn't married, lived alone. Why would she be secretive?

He waited a few minutes before entering. Andrea's attention was fixed on the screen in front of her. Rossi walked a row behind, glancing at the screen over her shoulder. All he could see was the open.com email logo on it. That was enough for him to suspect secret communication. But with whom? he wondered.

Rossi left the cafe and positioned himself across the street, waiting for Andrea's next move. About 20 minutes later, he saw her leaving the cafe. He followed her back to her building. She went inside. Then he went back to the cafe.

Under the guise of being interested in meeting the young lady he saw earlier, Rossi asked the kid at the counter if he remembered whether she came in regularly, saying he wanted to plan to "accidentally" run into her again. The kid hesitated a little and looked askew at Rossi.

"Not sure, man. Lotta people come in. Are you a cop, or something?" the kid asked with attitude.

Rossi let that go and slipped a $5 bill across the counter, "What day and what time does she usually come in? That's all I need to know.

The kid looked down, took the bill, and said, "She comes in every couple of weeks, usually a Monday or Tuesday, I think. Looks like she's coming from work, so I guess around 5:30 or 6. I'm here from 3 to 11, so that's all I know."

Back on the street, Rossi pulled out his small notebook and wrote:

Andrea Manetti — Open.com login at public café. Computer at home.
Something to hide?
Terminal #3. Possible contact.

This wasn't over. Not by a long shot.

Armed with more information on her movements, Rossi headed home with a plan.

CHAPTER 26

THE DIGITAL THREAD

THE Trenton Police Department's Fraud "Bunco" Squad occupied the far end of the second floor in an aging municipal building with cracked linoleum and government-issue furniture. The squad's bullpen was cluttered but organized— in that chaotic way veteran cops understand. Folders were stacked in leaning towers, corkboards dotted with mugshots of international conmen, screenshots of websites, and examples of email scams.

Sgt. Charlie Capobianco sat at his desk beneath a humming fluorescent light, one hand gripping a chipped coffee mug that read: *Fraud Happens*. He looked the part: late fifties, thick neck, thinning hair slicked straight back, a tie knot halfway down his chest like he stopped caring two decades ago.

His desk phone, beige with a coiled cord, rang.

"Sergeant Capobianco," he barked, not looking up.

"Cappy, it's Rocky."

"Hey paisano," Capobianco grinned, recognizing the voice instantly. "Still chasing phantoms for that insurance company?"

"Yeah, Brooklyn office. Mostly, I work from home now. Get

my assignments and only go in a couple of times a month. Less of a grind. Occasionally, an interesting puzzle turns up."

"You always liked puzzles. And hey, how's the kid, your grandson—he still blowing through your pension money on video games?"

"Worse. Now he wants to go to dance school. I told him I'd rather buy him a car. No, seriously, I'll foot the bill for lessons. He's a good kid, ya' know."

They laughed. For a minute, it was like they were leaning against a patrol car again, swapping stories and bad jokes.

"We gotta grab a beer soon, hit the dart board at the F.O.P. I still got the trophy you never won."

"Yeah, yeah. Listen, I need a favor—tech-related."

Capobianco leaned back in his chair, eyes narrowing. "Oh boy. Whenever a guy your age says 'tech,' I get nervous. What kind of favor?"

Rossi's voice dropped a notch. "I'm working a possible fraud. Guy presumed dead from 9/11. His sister's the beneficiary. Something smells off. Word is he got himself involved with some wiseguys on Long Island. I caught her at a public internet café using an email account—*open.com*. Might be communicating with the 'dead' guy. I want to know if there's a way to intercept what she's doing."

Capobianco blew out a long breath. "Jesus, Rocky. You sure know how to pick 'em."

"Cappy, this one's weird. She filed the claim fast. Too fast. I'm not sensing the grief I've seen from some other 9/11 family members. Then there's the email thing. She's got a full computer setup in her apartment, but she goes outta her way to use a beat-up machine in a Broadway café. With the mob connection and the FBI looking into him I'm wondering if he's on the run from the mob or the Feds, or both. The terror attack could be convenient under the circumstances."

Capobianco rubbed his chin. "Alright. First, you didn't hear this from me, and second—what you're asking for is about one toe over the line, and one foot in federal court."

"I know the risk," Rossi said. "I'll play it careful. Just need to see if there's something there. If there is, I'll figure out another way to surface it."

Capobianco rolled his eyes. "You always were good at threading the needle."

He opened a drawer, fished out a small black flash drive, and twirled it in his fingers.

"We've been testing these things called keyloggers on court-authorized cases. Fancy name, simple job. You plug it into a terminal, and it sucks up every keystroke stored in the computer's RAM. It even captures login names and passwords—if you're lucky and quick."

"How quick?" Rossi asked.

"The data hangs around for a short time, while the computer is processing. Sometimes it's good until the machine's rebooted. Depends on how old the computer is. So, if you wait too long or they power it down, you're outta luck."

"What's the process?"

Capobianco got technical but kept it street-level. "Plug it in. Auto-executes. You'll see a prompt, hit enter, and it dumps the keystrokes into a secure partition, then onto the flash drive. Eject the drive, walk out clean. Later, on your own machine, open the file, the drive will unencrypt the code. Then scroll through everything the user typed—login credentials, passwords, other text, even access to emails. Even deleted stuff, sometimes."

"Jesus Christ," Rossi muttered. "It's like cracking a safe with a toothpick."

Capobianco grinned. "Yeah, welcome to modern surveillance. We could've used one of these in '98 with that dry cleaner on Hamilton who ran the numbers."

"How do I get one?"

"I don't know what you're talking about," Capobianco said flatly, standing to stretch his back. Then, more softly, "But, say hi to your mailman for me."

Rossi smiled. "You're a prince, Cappy."

"If this comes back to me, I'll deny it in three languages."

Rossi chuckled. "Appreciate it. And I'll bring the darts next time."

"You buy the beer," Capobianco replied, hanging up the phone.

CHAPTER 27

GROUND ZERO WEST

I was just after 8 a.m. when Rocco Rossi left his modest duplex in Trenton and headed east in his aging maroon Chevy Caprice toward Staten Island. He took Route 1 north, then merged onto the New Jersey Turnpike, passing refineries and the large cranes that towered over Newark Bay. Traffic slowed near the Goethals Bridge, but by 9:30, he was across and driving down Arthur Kill Road toward Fresh Kills, the sprawling landfill-turned-crisis-site now known among insiders as Ground Zero West.

Previously, visitors to the landfill would first encounter towering heaps of household garbage and seagulls circling lazily above the dump like sentries. Now, just beyond the gate stands a temporary command post—rows of prefabricated trailers and canvas-wrapped structures run by a joint task force of the NYPD, FBI, and FEMA. The air still carried the sour smell of dust and chemical smoke from Ground Zero debris, which was trucked and barged in load by load from lower Manhattan. A distant mechanical hum emanated from heavy excavators moving rubble in quadrant grids—a grim ballet of machines turning over ash and twisted metal searching for clues and closure.

Rossi showed his investigator ID to the National Guard checkpoint guard. "Claims Division, Trinity Life and Casualty. Here to follow up on a WTC case."

"Head to the Personal Effects trailer," the guardsman said, pointing toward a structure flanked by two green FEMA tents. "Ask for Corporal Kupinski."

Inside the trailer, a young, clean-shaven NYPD corporal in fatigues, boots, and a military haircut stood behind a gray metal desk under harsh fluorescent light. He looked fresh-faced but carried the serious posture of a man shouldering a sacred duty. Probably a former Marine, Rossi speculated.

"You Kupinski?" Rossi asked.

"Yes, sir," the corporal replied, standing to greet him. "Corporal Viktor Kupinski, NYPD, sir. How can I help you?" Kupinski replied."

Rossi nodded. "Appreciate your service, corporal. Did you volunteer for this duty?"

"Yes, I did, sir."

Definitely Marine, Rossi thought.

"I'm following up on a possible ID match—name's Michael Manetti. Supposed to have perished on 9/11. I'm trying to confirm any personal effects."

Kupinski entered the name into the alphabetical computer file listing personal items recovered. "Manetti..." as he repeated the name. "Here it is. One item recovered. No confirmed remains," as he scanned the file. "Just a briefcase and contents."

He scribbled a retrieval slip and handed it to an assistant. "It'll take a bit to retrieve it. Items are filed in quadrant storage—code

9-R. You're welcome to wait in the break tent."

Rossi stepped outside. The morning sun had broken through the clouds, but the air remained damp from the nearby marsh and ash. From his vantage point, he watched the surreal rhythm of forensic teams in Tyvek suits inspecting steel beams, hunched over grids marked by colorful flags. Machines and handlers sifted through bucket-loads of twisted debris.

Suddenly, work stopped in the recovery section closest to the Personal Effects trailer. The workers paused silently as a firefighter's helmet was recovered. They all removed their helmets and bowed their heads. Some wept. Some crossed themselves.

Rossi immediately understood. He bowed his head in silence.

Thirty minutes later, Kupinski's assistant flagged him down. "We've got the item. Follow me."

Rossi signed the chain-of-custody form on a clipboard and entered a side room set up like a forensics lab. On the table, inside a transparent evidence bag, was a scuffed, expensive oxblood leather briefcase, dusty and warped, with the gold-embossed initials *M.J.M.* still visible below the handle. The clasp had been broken clean through.

"Found in good condition, considering," the officer noted.

Rossi unzipped the bag. The faint smell of concrete dust mixed with aged leather.

Inside:

- A waterlogged Day-Timer™ with a black vinyl cover
- A plastic bottle of antacid tablets
- Two ball-point pens
- A yellow legal pad with scribbled notes and financial figures

- Three client folders
- And a glossy travel brochure for Key West

The officer leaned in. "Looks like standard office gear. Any significance?"

Rossi flipped to the Day-Timer's address section. A name jumped out: *Sonny Patrilla.*

He didn't react, just nodded, as he scanned the calendar pages. Notations for dinner meetings, client calls, and then—under September 7— *"Spring Lake, Sally. Res. confirmed."* Rossi flipped forward to September 11. *"8:30—Ralph, coffee shop."*

Ralph, who's Ralph? Rossi thought to himself. *Could be something. Maybe nothing.*

He turned the travel brochure over. On the back, a handwritten note: *"We talked about this. Maybe for a February vacation?"* signed with just a capital *S.*

Rossi opened one of the manila folders marked *"Usher."*

The documents seemed to be complex international bank transactions, including bank statements, account names and numbers, transaction amounts, dates, and invoices.

Maybe the feds could make something of this, Rossi thought.

He turned to the officer. "Can you show me the recovery location data?"

The officer checked the evidence slip. "Code 10221415-S35. That's October 22nd, 2:15 p.m., grid S-35."

He directed Rossi to a wall map with a checkerboard overlay. "S-35," the officer translated and pointed to the map, "runs from Liberty Street up to the southern lobby entrance of Tower Two. If the briefcase was found in that range, it could've been dropped outside during the initial chaos."

"Why do you say that?"

"Well, from what I've heard from some of the recovery crew, as the upper floors collapsed upon the lower floors, the falling debris pushed the perimeter outward. Something falling that close and found so late could have hit the concrete early in the collapse."

Rossi nodded and thought to himself... *Manetti's office was in the North Tower. Was his meeting in the North Tower, the South Tower, or somewhere else? If it was in the North Tower at 8:30, why was he in the vicinity of the South Tower later? He could have left the South Tower before or after it was hit, or maybe never gone inside the tower at all.*

He shook the officer's hand. "Thanks, officer. This helps."

The Caprice rumbled back onto the Staten Island Expressway as Rossi replayed it all in his mind:

- The briefcase was found on the sidewalk or in the street, probably early in the collapse.
- A brochure mentioning Key West.
- No other notes in the Day-Timer™ indicating non-business travel
- A meeting that morning with someone named Ralph.
- A name known to be of interest to the FBI, Sonny Patrilla.
- Client files that could contain incriminating information on money laundering.

Where the briefcase was found, under the rubble, pointed to a single possibility: Manetti may have never died in the towers. He may have walked away that morning... and used the chaos as his chance to disappear.

Rossi gripped the wheel tightly.

Now I need what Andrea won't give me. And I need that keylogger.

CHAPTER 28

THE REVELATION OF COMPLICITY

THE news came in fragments. Headlines. Statements. Surveillance photos. Then the names.

The FBI released all nineteen.

Manetti, in his motel room, studied the faces on the TV screen like mug shots from another world—some blurred, all young, none of them familiar.

Until one was.

Hani Hanjour.

Saudi national. Twenty-nine years old. AA Flight 77. Hijacker Pilot. The Pentagon.

He remembered the face. And the name.

It was eight months ago. A meeting set up by Willoughby. A routine ask for an important client.

"Help this young man get settled. He's here on a student visa and needs cash for travel, tuition, and living expenses. His name is Hani Hanjour. He is being assisted by Ziad Abdullah. Here are the details," Willoughby instructed Manetti while handing him the information.

The client was Ziad Abdullah, the Saudi billionaire with businesses in South America and Africa; ore mining, oil exploration, diamonds, and gold, things people died for. Officially, a mining magnate. Unofficially, a man whose companies moved more than just rock.

Abdullah was one of Willoughby's prized connections. Enormous wealth. Saudi royal family adjacent. Untouchable. Manetti never asked questions.

Willoughby delegated more of Abdullah's business dealings to Manetti, making him mainly responsible for overseeing dozens of shell companies on behalf of Abdullah enterprises. Willoughby took advantage of Manetti's special skills in disguising transactions to dodge taxes and regulatory scrutiny.

Manetti assembled $500,000 in cash and a debit card linked to an offshore blind account. It was what they did. Deniable, untraceable, all aboveboard—on paper.

He remembered Hanjour's handshake. Polite. Curious.

"What do Americans think of Islam?"

"Is it true New Yorkers are rude?"

"Have you ever been in a small plane?"

They talked about movies.

He liked *The Godfather*. Said *Die Hard* was overrated.

He asked if you needed good English to learn to fly.

Then he was gone. And now he was back.

On every screen.

A killer.

******

Manetti sat still. The motel walls around him felt too close.

He remembered the man's smiling face, not the one from the news. Remembered handing him the briefcase to carry it all.

The sick weight hit him in the chest. Not like fear.

More like truth.

Willoughby couldn't have known, he told himself.

But hadn't he wondered?

Why that much cash? Why the urgency? Why a student with no apparent coursework, no university credentials?

Because it was never their job to ask. That was the deal. That was how they operated.

He didn't know.

And now it didn't matter.

CHAPTER 29

THE INSURANCE FILE

A T the end of the week, Andrea checked for any message from Michael.

A new draft was in the file.

Clear instructions for her to find and mail important files to him asap.

Andrea stepped off the M79 bus on Lexington into the December afternoon, clutching her tote bag close. The street was lively. Honking horns. Buses idling. The rich smell of roasted peanuts from the corner cart. Her nerves jittered in sync with the traffic.

Walking south on Lexington to 78th. Her brother's building stood as it always had—quiet, dignified, prewar. A doorman nodded to her as she entered the lobby.

The fifth-floor hall smelled of rich varnished oak and something faintly floral. She fished the spare key from her coat pocket, the key Michael had given her just months earlier, "just in case", he had said.

She unlocked the apartment.

And froze.

The place was in shambles.

Cushions sliced open. Desk drawers yanked. Books and papers scattered across the floor. A chair on its side, its underlining slit. Lamps knocked askew. Bed linens tossed to the floor. Her breath caught in her throat.

"Oh my God, Michael…"

She stood in the doorway for a moment, heart pounding. No sign of forced entry, no sign the intruder was still there. Just a mess. Whoever it was, they'd been thorough—and focused. Someone had been hunting for something.

She gathered herself and moved to the bedroom. Top dresser drawer. Top right, he said. Hands trembling, she felt along the underside.

There—taped to the wood. A small blue envelope, inside, a brass key.

She didn't stay long.

Back outside, she caught a cab heading south to Midtown. The banker at Lexington & 47th led her silently through the muted lobby with heels clicking the marble floor, to a small, curtained room on the vault level.

Andrea slid the key into Box 419. The banker inserted his copy. The lock clicked open.

Inside, on the bottom, and among personal items and official-looking documents, a single manila envelope. "INSURANCE" printed in Manetti's unmistakable handwriting.

She didn't open it.

The cab took her toward home, pulling over at the post office near Broadway. At a self-service kiosk, she paid and slid the envelope into a Priority Mail package, addressed it to:

Michael Manetti

c/o General Delivery

Key West, Florida 33040

On her walk home, she ducked into the Bytes & Beans Internet Café.

She logged into the email drop account.

Drafts empty.

She typed:

Michael—Your apartment was trashed. Someone was clearly looking for something. I was scared out of my mind, but I found the key and followed your instructions. The envelope is on its way.

But I need to know what all this means? Are you okay? Why are you doing this? What should I do about your place? I'm really scared.

Oh, a few days ago, when I returned to my apartment after Pilates, I thought I smelled cigarette smoke. Nothing seems askew, nothing notably missing, but I just had this funny feeling that someone had been in my place. Now this! Do you think there's a connection? What should I do?

She saved the draft.

Then logged out.

Beans & Bytes Café

Friday, Late Afternoon

The sky had already gone pewter-gray by the time Rossi parked on the side street across from Beans & Bytes. A harsh wind stirred garbage around the storm drains, whipping dead leaves past news racks and rustling the metal gate of the Korean deli next door. He left the engine and heater of his Chevy running and leaned forward, watching.

The café had become familiar by now, since he had been staking it out for the past two weeks. He was starting to recognize some of the regulars, even assigning them imagined identities, nicknames, and occupations. Behind the glass front, the green glow of computer monitors cast shadows onto the narrow walls. Kids with backpacks, a woman in scrubs, a man in a knit cap—all typing, scrolling, reading. But then he saw her.

Andrea Manetti approached the front door.

Rossi straightened up. His pulse ticked up, but he forced his breath to slow. For weeks he had waited, staking out the café from the car with coffee and cold knishes. And today, she showed.

Andrea pushed through the door in a wool coat, scarf tight against her neck, protecting against the wind. She didn't hesitate. She moved with purpose toward the back row of computers, selected terminal #3—same one he'd seen her use before—and logged in.

From his angle on the sidewalk, Rossi could just see her posture: upright, tense, alert. She was reading something. Her fingers twitched across the keyboard. Several minutes later, she stood and walked over to the printer.

She retrieved a single page.

He watched her pause, scan the document, fold it neatly, and slide it into her bag. Back at the terminal, she typed briefly, her brows furrowed with concentration. Then she logged off, gathered her belongings, and left as quickly as she arrived.

From the shadow of the adjoining store entrance, Rossi gave her ten seconds. Then he opened the cafe door.

A bell tinkled as he stepped inside. The heat hit him first—dry and recycled—but more comfortable than sitting in his car. The young clerk behind the counter barely looked up from his phone. If he recognized Rossi, he didn't show it.

Rossi made for terminal #3. Sat down. Pulled the flash drive from his jacket pocket.

The USB port was on the side of the monitor. He inserted it, careful not to attract attention. A moment later, a prompt appeared:

INSTALL?

He clicked it.

The screen blinked. A loading bar appeared—green dots blinking in sequence. Then:

COPY?

He hit the key. A hum from the drive. The green lights flickered rapidly, then stopped.

EJECT?

He tapped it. The flash drive stilled.

Rossi pulled it free and slipped it into the pocket of his leather jacket. He avoided eye contact and headed out, pushing through the door into the wind.

Back in the car, he allowed himself a grin. The drive had worked.

The ghost of Michael Manetti may have just left a trail of breadcrumbs—and Rocky Rossi was about to follow.

******

The flash drive in Rossi's pocket held something much more valuable than plastic and circuitry—evidence. After weeks of stakeouts, cold coffee, and restless Monday and Tuesday afternoons staring through Beans & Bytes' fogged windows, Andrea Manetti finally appeared.

Now, with the data freshly collected, Rossi didn't want to risk compromising the terminal where the keystrokes were logged. Instead, he ducked into a grungier internet café a block away, a forgotten relic squeezed between a Laundromat and a discount perfume shop. Inside, a row of terminals cast a pale green light across the room. The clerk, a bored teen with chipped black nail polish and a nose ring, didn't look up as Rossi fed quarters into a machine and claimed an empty seat.

Rossi slid the flash drive into the USB port. The terminal blinked awake, and he opened the file containing the keystroke log. It took a moment to parse, but scrolling down, there it was:

makefile

CopyEdit

Username: lazarus1

Password: TheBronx

He smirked. *Lazarus. A man returned from the dead. Clever.*

Navigating to *open.com*, Rossi entered the credentials. The inbox was empty. So was Sent Mail. Trash—nothing. Then, as he hovered over the **Drafts** folder, his gut twitched.

One message.

He clicked.

There it was—Andrea's words.

Rossi leaned back. So this is how you're doing it, he thought. Same inbox. Same login. No transmission. One writes, the other reads. Digital dead drop.

Andrea's message was ominous. *What is he running from?* Rossi thinks. *Who trashed his apartment? Could it be the Fed, or a threatened client? What were they looking for in Andrea's apartment? What did Andrea send? Manetti must know something that could threaten his life or put him in prison. Either is a motive to disappear.*

He jotted everything in his notebook and logged out, erased the browser history, then ejected the flash drive. On the way out, he passed a payphone outside and paused to dial.

An officer answered, "Trenton PD, detectives."

"Charlie Capobianco, please. It's Rocco."

The familiar gravel voice answered after two rings. "Rocky, you breathing heavy for a reason, or is that just your age catching up?"

Rossi chuckled. "Thanks for the tip, by the way." Surreptitiously thanking Cappy for the drive. "Got a question for you. Ever heard of perps using email drafts as drop points?"

There was a pause. "Yeah. It's a thing. Shared email account. Leave a draft, never send it. No trail, no metadata showing it ever left the inbox. One of our cyber kids flagged that trick last year. Got used in a wire fraud ring out of Queens. You trip on it from what I'm thinking?"

"I'll buy you a drink and explain it. For now, just confirm I'm not crazy."

"You're not crazy. Just a half-step ahead of the rest of us."

Rossi hung up and lit a cigarette, pacing beneath the café's flickering neon sign. The picture was becoming clearer: Michael Manetti had used 9/11 to disappear. But why? Who was after him? And now Andrea—clearly in deep—was helping him. Rossi didn't know what they were planning, but it was more than insurance fraud.

He made his decision: No need to follow Andrea. Manetti was probably out of Manhattan. He now had access to their communications. He had her voice in text. If he played it right, he could use that voice—those fears, doubts, and her desire to protect Michael—to turn her and to get to Manetti.

Back in Brooklyn, he'd set a schedule to check the Lazarus inbox every 48 hours. He wouldn't touch anything. Just watch. Wait. And when the time was right—he'd make his move.

******

Two Days Later – Key West

At the internet café off Caroline Street in Key West, the scent of sea salt and coffee mixed in the air. Michael Manetti logged in and saw her message waiting.

He read it twice.

Then typed:

Andi—You're brave, and I'm sorry. I never wanted you dragged into this. Don't go back to my apartment. Let it be. If anyone comes asking, you don't know anything. When you are out, or entering your building, just be vigilant of your surroundings. I'm sure, if someone was searching your place, they either found what they were looking for or not. In either case, I don't think they will be back. With what you have told me, I too, will be more vigilant.

Here's the truth. One of our firm's clients was directly tied to funding the attacks. He funneled money through shell companies I helped build. I even provided cash to a man named Hani Hanjour... You saw his photo. He flew the plane into the Pentagon.

I didn't know anything about him. But that doesn't change what I did. I helped the machinery function. I can't live with that.

What I'm doing now—it's for them. For the people who jumped from windows. For their families. The files you mailed are part of something bigger. I need them to finish what I started. Someone needs to bring light to the truth buried deep in the rubble.

Don't worry about me. Just be safe. If you need to reach me, you know how. I love you.

He saved the message as a draft. Deleted hers.

Then he logged off and leaned back against the chair; the whir of the ceiling fan was his only company.

The Weight of Truth

Later that afternoon, as the sun hung low and cast slats of light across the weathered Venetian blinds, Rocco Rossi sat alone in Trinity Life & Casualty's Brooklyn office. The old desk creaked beneath his forearms as he powered up the office desktop—a bulky Dell tower rescued from obsolescence, much like the rest of the furniture in Cal Winters' Claims Inquiry Department.

The others had left for the day. The building was quiet but for the sound of the cleaning lady's cart as she moved down the corridor, and the occasional honk from street traffic. Rossi inserted the flash drive, navigated to the *open.com* login screen, and typed:

Username: *Lazarus1*

Password: *TheBronx*

The screen flickered once before the dashboard loaded.

Nothing in the inbox.

Nothing sent.

One message sat quietly in the **Drafts** folder.

He clicked it open.

And read.

Andi—You're brave, and I'm sorry...

His eyes narrowed as the words spilled out. The breath caught in his throat halfway through the second paragraph.

One of our firm's clients was directly tied to funding the attacks. He funneled money through shell companies I helped build. I even provided cash to a man named Hani Hanjour... You saw his photo. He flew the plane into the Pentagon.

Rossi sat back, stunned.

This wasn't just an insurance scam or a missing-person case. This was something else entirely. *Terrorist funding. Hani Hanjour. Simon & Kershaw.* The implications were too vast to grasp in one sitting.

He re-read the message twice. Then a third time. Each pass peeled back another layer. Manetti wasn't innocent, no—he admitted as much. He was a cog in someone else's machine, a facilitator.

And now, he was trying to make it right.

What I'm doing now—it's for them. For the people who jumped from windows. For their families. ... I need [the files] to finish what I started.

Rossi slowly pushed back from the desk. The chair let out a groan under his weight. He rubbed his temples, the headache forming like a storm on the horizon.

What the hell did I just walk into? Rossi thought.

His mind reeled:

- *If Manetti's telling the truth, this confession is beyond my pay grade.*
- *He'll have a target on his back.*
- *What is he planning?*
- *And Andrea—she's my only chance.*

Rossi glanced at the message one last time, then hit **Print**. The old Epson chattered to life in the corner, slowly spitting out the single page like it knew it was giving birth to something radioactive.

He pulled the sheet, folded it crisply, and slid it into an unmarked file in his locked drawer. He didn't yet know who to give it to—FBI, Justice, hell, maybe even the *Times.* But one thing was clear:

He had to find Manetti.

And to do that, he'd need Andrea.

He couldn't come in hard. Not this time. No cop's glare, no rapid-fire questions. She wouldn't respond to that. She loved her brother—Rossi had seen that in her eyes. But now, that love could be used to build a bridge instead of a wall.

He'd frame it right: *Michael's in danger. Everyone's after him. You're the only one who can help me protect him.* That would be his opening.

Rossi stared at the screen for a long time before logging out and pulling down the blinds. He'd stepped into something far bigger than insurance. Bigger than mob families. This was national security. He was in it now—knee-deep in a truth few people would want to hear.

Could I be getting sucked into a conspiracy theory? It's too early to involve the Feds. I need more data for this story to be believed, Rossi mulled.

He switched off the monitor and reached for his coat.

Time to have a serious talk with Andrea Manetti. Time to change the terms of this conversation.

CHAPTER 30

SHADOWS AND CONSEQUENCES

THE West End Diner was the kind of place that hadn't changed since the early 70s; chrome-rimmed counter stools, laminated menus with fading color photos of blueberry pancakes and meatloaf specials, and a constant background of clinking plates and clattering utensils. In a throwback to even earlier times, a bell jingled over the door each time a new customer walked in or out.

Rocco Rossi was already in a corner booth facing the door. He nursed a black coffee, cracked open a packet of Sweet 'N Low, and kept an eye on the street.

Andrea arrived five minutes late, wearing a charcoal coat over slacks and a blue scarf tucked into the collar. Her movements were tense but composed, her face alert but drawn.

He raised his hand and stood. "Miss Manetti—Andrea. Thank you for coming."

She slid into the bench seat opposite him. "You said it was important?"

"It is. And I appreciate your time." He waited until the waitress poured coffee and shuffled off before speaking. "What I'm about to tell you might be hard to hear, but I want you to know—it's not coming from a place of judgment. Just facts. And concern."

Andrea stared at him, then nodded slowly. "Go on."

Rossi leaned in slightly. "Michael may be alive."

Her eyes didn't flinch, but her jaw set tight. "What makes you say that?"

"I can't share all the details. But... I've seen some things that lead me to believe he may have survived. And that he's gone into hiding."

"I filed the insurance claim in good faith. He was in the Towers."

"Right. But he also had reasons to disappear. There's reason to believe your brother was aware of an FBI probe into his law firm, Simon & Kershaw. One of their clients, Anthony Patrilla, is suspected of laundering money through shell corporations set up by someone in the firm, and maybe, with some control, by your brother."

Andrea kept still, lips pressed thin.

"I'm not saying Michael was guilty of anything violent. But he might've known too much. The kind of stuff that gets a man killed if the wrong people think he's going to talk. If he bolted, it might not have been to escape justice... but to survive."

"Are you suggesting Michael is running from the Patrilla family?"

"I'm saying it's possible. I used to work Major Crimes in Trenton. I've seen how people like Sonny Patrilla operate. They don't just clean house—they erase it. And if Michael was a threat to them..."

Andrea crossed her arms. "What are you really after, Mr. Rossi? This sounds more like a criminal investigation than an insurance one."

"It's both now," he replied bluntly. "I'm thinking that Michael may be using the insurance claim as a ruse, to show that he is dead, not necessarily to defraud us. And I can understand that. Don't say anything, but if you're in communication with Michael—if—then what started as a tragedy could turn into fraud. You could be implicated. And I don't want that for you. I get it—you're trying to protect your brother. But the truth is, people like Sonny Patrilla don't let go once they think someone's a loose end.

She looked away, out the window, watching a delivery truck backfire and roll past. Andrea replayed her suspicions of someone entering her apartment…and the scene in Michael's apartment only a few days ago. What Rossi was telling her began to make sense.

"I'm not the enemy here," Rossi said, his voice softer. "I want to help Michael. And you. But I need you to trust me. If Michael talks to me—even off the record—it could open doors. It might even save his life."

Andrea turned back to him, uncertain, but with a spark of something—curiosity, perhaps. Or doubt.

"You're asking me to betray him," she said, tipping her hand to the astute investigator.

"No," Rossi said. "I'm asking you to help him come out of the dark before someone else finds him first."

He pulled out a card and placed it on the table. "I'm a cop at heart. I've seen innocent people get into trouble that could have been avoided. I'm not saying Michael is totally without guilt, but that is not for me to say. Call me if he's willing to talk. I'll keep him safe. You have my word."

Andrea picked up the card, slid it into her purse as she walked out the door, without another word.

Later That Day – Beans & Bytes Internet Café

Andrea stepped out of the cold and into the warmth of the café. The barista gave a nod of recognition but didn't interrupt her pace. She headed to Terminal 3—the same one she always used—and logged into the *Lazarus 1* email account.

She opened the draft folder and began to type.

Michael—

I met with the insurance investigator again today. His name is Rossi. He's a former Major Crimes detective. He knows more than he's saying. He suspects you're alive. I didn't tell him anything. But I'm scared. I think he's serious about helping. He says you could be in danger—not just from the law, but from Patrilla.

Please, Michael. Think about contacting him. He seems honest... and determined.

I'll wait for your reply.

—Andi

She saved the message in draft, logged out, and walked home with her head down.

Monday – Rossi's Office

Rossi had been checking the Lazarus account twice daily now. This time, the draft folder had been updated.

Andi—

I understand. You did the right thing.

For now, maybe withdraw the claim. Say you're not ready to give up hope. That buys us time. I'll think about this over the next few days. I love you.

—M

Rossi leaned back in his chair, staring at the screen, thinking: He's alive. He's conflicted. And he might be ready to talk. Can I live up to my promise to Andrea? he thought.

Tuesday Morning

At the Key West post office on Whitehead Street, a pale clerk handed Manetti a red, white, and blue package.

Priority Mail. Manhattan return address.

He took a taxi back to the motel with the envelope under his arm. Whatever came next—this was the fuse.

He stared down at the flash drive he retrieved from his apartment two months ago, still secure in a pocket of his go bag. He picked up the envelope retrieved earlier from the central Key West post office. It was light. Too light for what it carried.

Inside the manila envelope: documents and a flash drive— more bank codes, shell companies, freeport accounts. The secret assets of men like Ziad Abdullah.

And Sonny Patrilla.

And the criminals who treated rare art as pawns in a world of greed, corruption, and duplicity. A world of old paintings and new favors.

He had built a digital mausoleum of some of the world's worst money. All hidden beneath initials and cross-registered shell companies with empty desks and post office boxes in places like Nassau, Tortola, Liechtenstein.

Freeports around the world filled with art never meant to be publicly seen again. Storage contracts for "museum-grade items." Fraudulent invoices for antique statuary and paintings to be displayed in private mansions and palaces.

He never asked where the art came from. Never asked who the buyers or sellers were. Some of it, he knew, was stolen. Some suspected Nazi loot, Middle Eastern tomb-plundered, and African tribal relics. Stolen culture.

But his fees cleared. That was the game.

He had helped them do it. All of them.

The criminals. The predators.

Even the terrorists.

He wasn't a victim.

He was a link in a chain.

A very well-paid one.

Now the game felt different.

******

The next morning, Manetti sat on the only chair in his room and watched the TV. Across the screen appeared a long and steady stream of dump trucks carrying debris and remains, heading to Staten Island for sifting and sorting.

The news hadn't changed much in weeks; bodily remains pulled from rubble, photos of the confirmed dead, funerals with no remains.

He read the names. Watched the faces. The little smiles meant for graduation photos or dating profiles. Now part of history. His history.

Then the name *Ralph Collucci* appeared in the *NY Times*, which he bought that morning at the newsstand.

Remains found. A short bio.

Manetti felt a weight press into his chest. Ralph had been more than a friend. He was a constant. Since their teens in The Bronx. Since Wallace's car wash. Since the gold refinery and the hustle. The kind of friend who remembered who you were before the money.

They'd shared secrets, schemes, and history.

And now Ralph was gone.

He probably perished just a few feet behind him in the darkness when the South Tower was hit. They lost each other on the stairway. Maybe Ralph stopped to help someone. Maybe he never made it up at all.

It was the most personal loss Manetti had known since his mother's passing.

Then his mind turned to Sally. Weeks earlier, her name ran beside the cropped photo—young, bright-eyed, full of everything she'd never get to become.

She had smiled at him on the 76th floor that fateful day. Spring Lake felt like another lifetime.

Sally had made him feel emotions at first not recognized. The first woman since he came to Simon & Kershaw who didn't just want diamonds and the brownstone address. She saw something real under the power veneer.

He thought about what might have been. And now she was gone too.

He closed his eyes. Images came uninvited—the fireball in the lobby, the screaming woman he'd carried, the darkness swallowing the towers.

The grief wasn't loud. It sat cold and tight in his gut. Made the coffee in his cup and the images in his head bitter.

He leaned back in the chair and stared at the ceiling, his jaw clenched, his throat dry.

He'd always told himself the crimes were victimless. That it was just the IRS. Just loopholes.

Just the rich protecting what was theirs.

But he saw it differently now.

There were always victims.

He sat there for a long time. Thinking of what Andrea said. About this detective, Rossi.

There had to be a reckoning.

Not for the dead.

For the living.

For him.

******

The manila envelope. With all its secrets, it held something else. Maybe... a way to make it right.

He thought about Hani Hanjour. The photo of his face in the paper.

That same face had sat in front of Manetti eight months ago. The "Saudi student," Willoughby said, needed help settling in. Referred and funded by Ziad Abdullah, the firm's prized client.

Now, that same young man had flown a plane into the Pentagon.

And Manetti, unknowingly, had greased the wheels.

Simon & Kershaw—through Willoughby —helped him do it.

Something about the encounter with Hanjour made Manetti uneasy at the time. So, he decided to document the assignment.

The envelope contained that explosive documentation –

incriminating evidence on Willoughby and Manetti's work for Abdullah. Willoughby's order to accumulate $500,000 cash and debit cards for Hanjour, the day's visitor log with Hanjour's name, the date of his visit, and who he was meeting.

Now the gray space of Manetti's "victimless crimes" was turning black.

And blood red.

******

The firm was gone. The office, a charred tomb. The FBI had bigger targets for now—international terrorist cells, border watchlists, visa overhauls, and transportation security. If he stayed quiet, if Andrea held the line, the feds might not come looking again, for a while.

And, what about this detective Rossi? Manetti thought. He would not put Andrea at risk for filing the claim. He couldn't let that happen.

Could he live with the guilt of knowing his and Willoughby's involvement with Hanjour?

And Willoughby was still unaccounted for.

That part unsettled him. If Willoughby had survived and been talking, it could shift everything. And Willoughby wasn't made of iron. He'd fold if it came to saving his own skin.

Which made Manetti's next move more urgent.

He had a name—E. Dean Broussard. A clean passport. A new life already in motion.

But was running enough? He didn't want to just disappear.

He wanted to *do* something.

Revenge. Restitution.

Justice maybe.

Redemption, even.

The files could bring the hammer down on Abdullah's complicity.

Maybe even use it to help the people who'd been hurt along the way.

He didn't know what that looked like yet.

But it was the first time in years he'd thought about *doing good*, not just making money.

He clasped the envelope closed and stepped out into the Key West light.

Salt in the air. Laughter from a bar nearby. A dog barking up the street.

A breeze passed over him.

He didn't know where the road would lead.

But it wasn't back.

Not anymore.

CHAPTER 31

A DAY OF REVIVAL

MANETTI showed up at the dock just after sunrise. He decided to take up Jim's offer made at dinner a couple of weeks ago. And Emily made a convincing argument.

The harbor was quiet except for the slap of tide against hulls and the caw of gulls circling the dumpster.

Captain Jim glanced up from tying off a bucket of chum. "Well, look at this. 'Morning, Dean. Glad you came. Had a bet with Em"

"Who won?"

"You won't get that from me," Jim laughed.

"Thought I could use some salt air," Manetti said. "Maybe a little humility."

Kenny grunted, "We've got both."

Kenny gave a nod from the deck of the *Kitty Jo*; chin tucked like always. "We'll find a job for him, Cap," thinking at the same time, *Suspicious. New Yorker.*

Manetti grinned. "I've never been on a fishing boat. I'll follow orders and try not to throw up."

He boarded the *Kitty Jo*, a thirty-seven-foot Viking Sportfisher with scuffed sides and good bones. Diesel rumble, hot coffee, and sea salt in the air.

Four guys from Indiana were the day's charter. High school buddies turned middle-aged dads chasing big water stories.

Kenny handed Manetti a rag and a rule: "Don't get in the way, and don't fall overboard."

They motored out over glassy water, the sky a sweep of rose and blue. As they passed Mallory Square, the cruise ship horns groaned like beasts waking. The scent of diesel mingled with seaweed and baitfish.

They hit the reef first. Manetti passed bait and beers, learned how to handle the gaff, and smiled when one of the Hoosiers hooked a snapper big enough to require two hands.

"You're good luck," one of them told him. Manetti just nodded.

Later, they moved into deeper water, trolling for kingfish. Lines sang and reels screamed as a forty-inch fighter tore a hole in the Gulf and gave everyone a show.

By late afternoon, the wind kicked up. Jim began a slow turn back to port.

"Squall coming," Jim said, scanning the western sky. He throttled up. "Lines in."

But not fast enough.

The rain hit like a wall; horizontal, hot, and blinding. Swells lifted *Kitty Jo* two, three feet off rhythm. One of the Indiana guys went down hard against the gunwale.

"Jesus, my arm," he hissed.

Manetti was there fast, pulling him to the bench, wrapping an iced towel around the limb. "Don't move it. You're okay."

Kenny lashed down the gear. Jim rode the throttles like he was breaking a horse. Manetti caught himself thinking this was how a man earned his sea legs—wet, grimy, scared, and useful.

The storm passed fast. Most in the Gulf do. The rain cut off like a faucet and left the water flat and steaming. When the hurt man insisted he could manage, Jim nodded. "Fishing's done. Still looking stormy in the West. We're heading in."

Back at the dock, the air was thick with salt and humidity. Gulls screamed overhead. Fish blood slicked the planks underfoot.

While the guests strolled up the dock toward a cook-your-catch restaurant, Kenny and Manetti stayed behind. The boat had to be scrubbed.

"You're on fish boxes," Kenny said, tossing him gloves and a stiff brush.

Manetti didn't argue.

The work was raw and real. He scooped out melted ice, guts, and scales—his nose burning from the brine and the iron-rich smell of blood. His skin sunburnt. He could hear Kenny's hose spraying down rods and reels, the slap of gear stowing beneath deck.

Jim checked the bilge pumps, opened the engine hatch, and filled a notepad with tomorrow's prep list. It was like watching a man maintain an organism, not a boat.

Kenny showed Manetti how to coil lines. Scrub the rail. Haul bait buckets. The scents stuck—sun-dried bait, rust, old rope, sweat.

He liked the work more than he could have imagined.

Later, at the Fisherman's Net, Manetti nursed a cold beer beside Kenny, retelling stories of the day.

Emily walked in, hair wind-tangled from her bike ride after

work at R.E.E.F.S., and having stopped by the charter office before coming to the Net. The bar stirred when she arrived—like it always did.

"Well, Eli," she said, sliding onto the stool beside him. "How'd you like your first full shift?"

Manetti lifted the bottle. "Tired, soaked, sore... and oddly satisfied."

Kenny chuckled. "That's called a real job."

Emily smiled, then handed Manetti a small envelope. "Split from today's trip."

He opened it—$100 in twenties.

"Wait—this is too much. I was a liability."

"You worked," Kenny said with authority. "That counts."

Manetti tried to hand it back, but Kenny raised a hand. "We split tips. That's the rule."

"You guys are something else," Manetti said. "If you ever need a part-time deckhand who knows absolutely nothing, I'm your guy. At least I didn't puke."

They laughed.

Kenny moved to the pool table where his quarter was next on deck.

Manetti looked at Emily. "Apparently, I've come into some money. Can I take you to dinner tomorrow night?"

She met his gaze, then nodded. "Sure. I've got a favorite spot. My dad says their puttanesca's better than Naples."

"Perfect. It's a date then."

They smiled.

And for a brief moment—putting aside the guilt, the lies, and the ghosts of Ground Zero—Manetti felt like a man stepping into the light.

She stood, hesitated, then kissed him lightly on the cheek. "See you then, Eli.", turning her head toward him with a smile as she walked out into the warm Key West night.

And Manetti, still in sea-soaked shorts and the stink of fish on his skin, suddenly felt something settle inside him.

Not peace. Not yet.

But something…a direction.

A place to start.

CHAPTER 32

CONCH REPUBLIC

MANETTI arrived early. Khaki shorts, a new Tommy Bahama shirt, and boat shoes.

Carmella's Cucina was half-full, the kind of place where every table came with a red-checkered cloth and a story. Candles flickered in the necks of empty Chianti bottles, their wax pooled thick over the glass like dripped time. Behind the bar hung black-and-white photos of Italian families and olive groves. American flags shared space with Italian tricolors. Sinatra music was conspicuously absent. Carmella's husband would never fully explain.

Manetti took a stool at the bar. Ordered a Manhattan, rocks.

Emily walked in just past seven, and the noise of the room seemed to dim for a beat.

She wore a floral sundress that moved like a soft breeze. Her shoulders were golden from the sun, her hair loose and falling to her shoulders. Not done up. Just... herself. The kind of beauty born on the water, not in a mirror.

Manetti stood. She smiled when she saw him.

"You clean up nice," she said.

"I try."

They were seated at a table for two in the corner, beneath a mural of Positano. A candle glowed low between them.

The waitress addressed her by name. It's a small town.

She brought breadsticks and poured olive oil onto a saucer without asking.

Emily told stories. Life as a Navy kid. Her father's postings. The bases, the moves, the constant change. She spoke with fondness, but you could hear the cost beneath it.

"I guess I always felt... portable," she said. "Places didn't last. People didn't either."

"You landed here," Manetti said.

"Eventually." She smiled. "And I stayed."

He told her about growing up in The Bronx. The gold refinery. The car wash. Laughing at stories of strange characters in their lives. Just enough. He was careful not to crack the shell too wide.

She pointed out the little Conch Republic flag near the register.

"You've seen that around town, right? The conch shell in the middle of a stylized Sun?"

"I was going to ask."

She leaned closer over her wine. "Okay, so here's the story the way I've always heard it. Back in the early eighties, drug smuggling off the South Florida coast was out of control, and the state and feds wanted to crack down. Their solution was roadblocks—real ones—set up at points along the Overseas Highway up to Route 1 at Key Largo, and north at the Card Sound bridge. You can imagine how that went. Every local trying to get to or from the mainland could get stuck for hours. Grocery runs, doctor visits, just driving to work—it all turned into a nightmare."

Manetti raised a brow. "Sounds like a mess."

"More than a mess," she said. "It pissed people off. The protests started, and lawsuits too. Folks were saying it felt like the Keys weren't even part of the U.S. anymore, like we were our own little island nation." She grinned, her eyes projecting a mischievous glint. "So Key West, being Key West, they decided to prove the point in the loudest way possible—they staged a secession. Declared the Keys an independent nation.

"It was pure PR theater," she said. "But with teeth. And it worked."

Manetti smiled, looking into her eyes. "So, you folks just declared independence?"

"Yeah. And then declared war on the U.S."

"You're kidding."

"Well, for one minute." She laughed. "Then we surrendered. And asked for foreign aid. Soon after, the checkpoints came down."

He laughed too. "That's brilliant."

"It was pure Keys," she said. "Make noise. Make fun. Win the fight and throw a party."

They clinked wine glasses, sipped to the Conch Republic, split the pasta puttanesca, and let the night slip into something slower.

Toward the end of the meal, a space opened on the small dance floor. Emily slid from the table and reached for his hand.

Surprised, but pleased, he stood and took her hand.

They moved like they had done it before. A natural rhythm. Her hand resting on his shoulder, fingers lightly at the nape of his neck. His hand at her waist.

She leaned her head against his chest. His hand settled on the small of her back. They didn't speak.

Back at the Wharf Motel, Manetti unlocked the door with a quiet flick of the wrist. The walkway behind them had gone still. Their laughter from dinner lingered faintly in the space between them. It had thinned now, replaced by something heavier.

Desire. Not rushed. Certain. Present.

Inside, the room smelled faintly of salt air and the single bar of soap left on the bathroom sink. Manetti closed the door and turned to her.

She glanced at his scattered clothes. Duffel bag half open. Briefs on the chair.

"You live like a man on the run," she said with a half-smile.

He smiled back, but said nothing.

Emily stood there, her hair still wind-tossed from the walk back, sundress brushing above her knees, sandals loose in her fingers.

She smiled, enticingly, knowing.

He stepped toward her. She didn't back away.

They met in the center of the room, like two currents drawn by the same tide.

Her mouth met his with a slow insistence—warm, open, hungry. She pressed her body into him, hands moving under his shirt, tracing the lean muscle across his stomach, the tension at his waist.

The stumble of a button. The whisper of a zipper.

He lifted the straps of her dress over her shoulders. It slipped off like silk. She stood in the soft motel light in white lace panties, breasts firm, and sun-kissed skin still warm to the touch. The sun hadn't left her. She carried its heat.

He let his hands explore her back, her shoulders, her hips—memorizing the lines, the contours. She arched into him with a soft exhale as he kissed her neck, just beneath the ear. A place that made her shiver.

"Dean," she whispered.

He pulled her close again, and the bed behind them creaked under their weight.

The panties came off slowly, pushed to the foot of the bed. She held his gaze, steady and unashamed. Her skin was flushed, her breath short now. He kissed her collarbone, the hollow of her throat, and lower.

Her legs wrapped around his hips. They found a rhythm. Slow. Intimate. Bodies pressed tight. Breath against breath.

She guided his hand with hers, confidently, assuredly.

He listened to her gasps, matched her pace to the way her body moved beneath him. She pulled him deeper, and they moved together—wave over wave—until she moaned softly, head buried in his shoulder, and he followed moments later, gripping the sheet, his body undone.

They stayed that way for a long time.

Entwined. Spent. Sweating into the sheets.

The only sound was the breeze through the palms and the uneven tempo of their breathing.

Later, in silence, she curled into his chest. He kissed the crown of her head. Her hand traced lazy circles on his skin. Not speaking. Not needing to.

Although he had lied to her, just then, in that bed, with her leg draped across his and her breath slowing against his skin, it felt like the truth was beginning.

No promises.

Not yet.

But something true.

CHAPTER 33

A NEW DAWN

E MILY woke to the low murmur of a coffee machine sputtering and steaming.

The air in the room was heavy with sleep and the scent of skin and linen.

She stretched, her hand reaching out over warm sheets to the space where his body had been.

Manetti was across the room, back turned, shirtless, barefoot, quietly moving.

The morning light sliced through the blinds in pale stripes, dancing across his back.

The ceiling fan spun overhead—steadily, endlessly—whispering white noise that wrapped around the silence like gauze.

He turned and smiled.

"Coffee's ready," he said.

She sat up slowly, letting the sheet fall just enough, watching him walk toward her. He handed her the mug—warm, black, no questions asked.

"I'm not used to being served," she said, still a little hoarse with sleep. "I like it."

"You're easy to serve."

The coffee wasn't good, but it was perfect. Nothing artisanal. But it felt right. A quiet morning and breath-warmed sheets. She sipped, watching him.

"I didn't expect last night," he said, sitting at the edge of the bed. "But I'm glad it happened."

She smiled over the rim of her mug. "Do I look like I have regrets?"

He didn't answer with words, just reached over and took the cup gently from her hands. Set it on the nightstand.

Then he pulled her into him.

There was no rush this time. No heat of surprise or storm of longing. Just warmth. Familiarity. Want, softened by consent.

She leaned into his mouth. Kissed him deeper. Slower. Her body melted over his, a rhythm returning as natural as the tide.

She eased him back against the mattress, her thighs straddling his hips, her hands braced on either side of his shoulders. The sheet fell away. His hands moved to her waist, then up. Reverent, searching.

They moved together slowly, letting the minutes stretch.

The blinds fluttered with each pulse of a cool morning breeze.

The room breathed with them.

It wasn't about proving something or losing control. It was about holding something—keeping it from slipping away.

Her hair brushed his face as she leaned close, breath catching in soft moans between whispered nothings.

His hands anchored her hips. She rolled her hips into him,

watching his eyes, needing to feel seen. Wanted.

He whispered her name like it meant something more now.

And when they finished, she lay curled on his chest, eyes closed, fingers drawing circles across his ribs.

Peace. That's what this was. Not escape. Not distraction.

Not lust.

Just… peace.

They lay quietly for a while savoring the moments.

Then his voice, quiet. Hesitant.

"So… Kenny."

She blinked. The name pulled her from her cocoon, just slightly.

"Kenny," she echoed. Her tone held no shame. Only memory.

"You said you grew up together. He wanted this life. You're living it. Why not with him?"

She sat up, reached for her coffee. It was cooler now. Still drinkable.

"Kenny's a good man," she said. "He knows the sea. Loves it. Works hard. Always did. But his dream was smaller than mine."

She looked at him, trying to read if that sounded cold. It wasn't meant to be.

"I thought I'd get out. Do something bigger. Maybe start a marine conservancy or a research non-profit. Something that mattered. Then Mom died. Dad needed help. I came back."

She traced her finger along the rim of the mug.

"I thought maybe Kenny and I could pick up where we left off. But it didn't fit anymore. He never left this place, so he never changed. I did."

He didn't interrupt.

"I still want a life. A family, maybe. A career of my own. But I want more than just running charters and watching sunsets. I love this town. But I'm not done dreaming yet. I have more to do."

She turned to face him fully.

"That's why Kenny and I didn't work."

Manetti nodded, slowly. "It's hard when the story you thought you'd write doesn't match the life you live."

She searched his eyes. "You've had that too?"

His pause was long.

When he finally spoke, it was with weight.

"I think I'm still figuring it out," he said. "Still trying to turn the page."

She leaned in. Kissed him on the cheek.

"You've got time."

"We both do."

They finished the coffee in bed, limbs draped, breaths slow.

Outside, the town hummed to life.

Inside, they lingered—two people not pretending, not hiding.

Above, the fan kept spinning. Wrapped in her arms, his world was quiet for the first time in days.

For once, it wasn't about what he was escaping.

It was about what he and Emily might be building.

CHAPTER 34

RISING TIDES

THE bakery near the docks was quiet that morning. The kind of quiet you didn't want to break.

A sea breeze drifted through the open windows, catching the edges of sheer white curtains and lifting them like sails. The smell of warm cinnamon and rising bread mixed with the clean scent of salt air and sun-bleached wood. In the background, an old radio played a Jimmy Buffett ballad about slowing down and letting go.

Emily sat across from him, her elbows on the table, hands wrapped around a mug. She hadn't said much since they sat down. Manetti didn't push.

She was wearing the night before sundress; sunglasses perched atop her head. Her hair pulled back in a loose braid, was still damp from a shower. She looked like someone trying to stay calm while something slowly unraveled in her hands.

She stirred her coffee. Once. Twice. Then set the spoon down.

"I've been thinking," she said, finally.

He nodded.

"I'm worried about Dad. About the business."

He waited.

"After the attacks, everything slowed down. No one's calling. A couple of charters canceled this week. Even tourists already in town are staying close to shore." She glanced past him, out the window. "People are scared."

He followed her gaze toward the marina. The *Kitty Jo* swayed gently in her slip, the morning sun glinting off the deck hardware like scattered coins.

"A few years back, Dad had to borrow against the boat," Emily continued. "We were coming off a rough season. He didn't want to let Kenny go, didn't want to miss a payment on the house, so... he leveraged what he had."

She sipped her coffee.

"We were almost caught up. But if this keeps up... I don't know how long we can hold on."

Her voice wasn't panicked, just tired. Tired in a way that comes from carrying too much for too long.

"What's the balance?" Manetti asked, setting his cup down.

"Eighty," she said. "Maybe closer to eighty-five with interest."

"And the lender?"

"Gulf Coast Marine Lending. Fort Myers. There's a guy—Jeff Crenshaw. He's our contact. Comes down every few months to check in, take his own measure of things. He's not a bad guy, just... a bank guy."

Manetti nodded slowly.

"I might be able to help."

She looked up, confused.

"I don't mean paying it off," he said quickly. "I mean, helping navigate it. I've handled this sort of thing. Restructuring. Sometimes, all it takes is a different approach. A voice that doesn't sound desperate."

Emily tilted her head slightly.

"You'd do that?"

"For you."

Her gaze held his. Soft. Surprised.

He reached across the table, not for her hand, just palm up on the wood between them. An invitation.

"I'll keep it professional. If your dad's open to it, all I need is the loan paperwork. Terms. Contact info. That's it."

Emily nodded, slowly, taking his hand, "I'll talk to him."

They sat quietly for a while. The air around them had changed. Warmer, closer. Not because of the weather, but because of what was settling between them.

"This place," she said, after a while. "It's like a boat, you know?"

He raised an eyebrow.

"Takes on water fast when things get rough. Storms. Recessions. Stuff like this."

Manetti smiled faintly. "And somebody's gotta keep bailing."

Emily smiled too. But there was something deeper in her expression now. Not relief exactly. Something closer to permission. To let someone else help carry the load.

Across the room, the owner swept crumbs from the counter. Outside, a pelican skimmed low over the marina, gliding just above the glassy water.

Later, alone in his motel room, Manetti would plug in the flash drive marked *Abdullah Holdings*. He'd sit in the glow of the screen, scrolling through account codes and shell companies, thinking.

He'd remember Emily's face in that moment in the coffee shop—hopeful, tired, trusting—and thought: *Do I want to continue this charade with someone I'm falling in love with?*

CHAPTER 35

FIRE ON THE WATER

THE Key West coastline shimmered under the early afternoon sun, the heat mellowed by a breeze from the south. The *Kitty Jo* eased from her slip, the thrum of her Cummins diesel engine rolling beneath their feet like a heartbeat. Jim Foster stood proudly at the helm of the boat; her white hull trimmed with faded blue stripes and the scent of salt worked deep into the fiberglass. It would be a day to celebrate Dean's restructuring of the bank loan a week earlier.

Beside him, Emily leaned over the rail, barefoot and smiling, her ponytail snapping in the breeze. Manetti sat aft on a cushioned bench, sipping a Corona, watching the ibis in the mangroves drift by as the *Kitty Jo* cruised toward the reef.

By midafternoon, they anchored in a quiet cove near Big Pine. They snorkeled, floated over coral, and spotted stingrays and parrotfish. Laughter rang across the water as they climbed back aboard and passed around foil-wrapped sandwiches and cold beer from the cooler.

It was the most relaxed day Manetti could remember having in years.

As the sun tilted low in the sky, the *Kitty Jo* powered up again, heading out alone into deeper waters—cutting foam and making good speed toward Key West.

"Not a bad day for a banker and an old fisherman," Jim joked, grinning at Manetti, who raised his bottle in salute.

Then the mood shifted.

Jim's eyes narrowed as he motioned off starboard. "That boat's been following us for a while now."

Off the starboard quarter, a low, dark 24-foot speedboat with twin Yamaha 300s made an abrupt, aggressive move toward the *Kitty Jo*, coming uncomfortably close—then suddenly cutting directly across their bow.

The *Kitty Jo* rocked hard from the wake.

"What the hell was that?" Emily muttered, steadying herself.

"Faded numbers. No name," Jim said, tightening his grip on the wheel. "That's not good."

The boat circled—always keeping a parallel distance—still too close for comfort. Then, suddenly, it surged forward, coming along on the port side.

The man at the wheel stood. Sunglasses. Ballcap. Expressionless.

The glint of a shotgun.

"DOWN!" Jim bellowed.

BOOM!

The first blast pockmarked the hull just above the waterline. Fiberglass splintered. Emily dropped. Manetti hit the deck. Jim slammed the throttle. The *Kitty Jo*'s powerful engines approached flank speed as Jim maneuvered to outrun the attacker. Soon, the *Kitty Jo* was ten miles offshore, alone except for the attacker.

"Emily! Below deck! Grab the shotgun and a handful of shells—in the red case near the tackle locker!"

She didn't hesitate. She ducked below, reemerged seconds later, cradling a pump-action 12-gauge Remington, with five shells clenched in her fist. Her face was tight, eyes blazing.

"Load her!" Jim shouted as he spun the wheel hard to port.

"Dean!" Emily barked over the roar of wind and engine. "Emergency flare gun! Port locker—grab it, load it, and be ready!"

Manetti scrambled to the red compartment. The orange flare gun tumbled out, along with three fat rounds. His hands trembled as he snapped open the barrel, then jammed a shell into its chamber.

Another blast from the speedboat. **BOOM!**

The Plexiglas flybridge shattered overhead. Jim winced but didn't flinch.

"Flare's in!" Manetti shouted.

"Wait until we turn!" Emily yelled, sliding shells into the shotgun. "You'll get a clean shot on our next swing!"

Jim shouted over his shoulder: "I'm pulling starboard—hold your fire until he's close!"

The speedboat gained on them again. It drew even, close enough to see the grim set of the driver's mouth.

"NOW!" Jim shouted.

Emily popped up and fired. The shotgun bucked. The blast ripped across the space between them—the speedboat's side panel exploded in a spray of fading gelcoat.

Manetti stood shakily, flare gun in both hands. "Is this even going to work?"

"Lead it!" Emily shouted. "Aim ahead of the console or engines!"

The speedboat swerved wide to flank them again. Manetti aimed, squeezed the trigger.

FWOOSH—the flare screamed across the water, but went high, splashing harmlessly behind the attacker.

"He's circling again," Jim warned. "Closer this time!"

Emily racked the shotgun. "Dean! Again!"

Manetti loaded a second flare, steadied his arms.

The attacker closed—fifteen feet off, weaving starboard.

FWOOSH!

This time, the flare slammed into the top of the console, catching fire instantly.

The driver slapped at the flames. The boat veered erratically.

"Nice shot!" Emily yelled.

The speedboat came again. She fired the shotgun—another blast, this time smashing a hole near the bowline.

Manetti fired his third flare just as the boat surged alongside.

The flare struck the port outboard engine.

WHUMP.

Then—**BOOM**.

A fireball erupted. The speedboat bucked, aft tilted down, then began to sink stern-first.

Within 90 seconds, it was gone—just fire-slicked debris and smoke curling into the Key West sky. The unidentified debris washed out to sea. The sharks would finish off any human remains.

Silence.

Only the sea and the rumble of the *Kitty Jo*'s diesel filled the void.

Jim eased off the throttle. "Everyone okay?"

Emily nodded, breathing hard, sweat and soot on her brow.

"I'm good," she said, still clutching the shotgun.

Manetti sat back heavily, the flare gun dangling in his hands. "That was…"

"Targeted," Jim finished. "Who was that guy? What was that all about?"

Manetti looked out over the oily water. Stunned.

"I think… I was the target."

At that moment, he knew he had to take action. It was no longer just his life at stake. He would contact Rossi.

CHAPTER 36

SOUTHERN COVENANT

THE day after the attack on the *Kitty Jo*, Michael Manetti sat in the Key West internet café, still shaken from the day before.

He had decided: hiding wasn't enough. If Sonny Patrilla had sent a gunboat once, he would send worse the next time—and Andrea or the Fosters could pay the price.

So he drafted a note for his sister:

Andi—forward the message that follows to the claims investigator, Rocco Rossi.

No return address, no explanation—just send it exactly as written. Love you. —M.

Then he composed the second message—measured, direct—and left both in the Lazarus draft folder.

Three hours later, Andrea copied the text into a fresh e-mail and fired it off from Beans and Bytes.

E-mail forwarded to Rocco Rossi

Mr. Rossi—

I'm Michael Manetti. I possess detailed records of major money-laundering schemes run through Simon & Kershaw for the Patrilla organization. I believe those same people now want me dead.

Andrea says you can be trusted and could help me. We never intended insurance fraud; the claim will be withdrawn.

Can you meet me in Atlanta in two days? Send a cell number and your flight details. I'll pick a safe location once you land.

—Michael Manetti

Rossi's reply (30 minutes later)

Mr. Manetti,
Cell #: (555) 230-2865.
I arrive ATL Wednesday 15:25 on Delta 1187.
I'm interested in crimes, not policies. If you're serious, I'll listen.
—Rocco Rossi, Investigator, Trinity L&C

The Windsor Hotel Meeting

Christmas lights blinked outside the Atlanta Windsor Hotel on Peachtree Street. As Rossi pushed through the bar's paneled doors, the scent of cinnamon garlands mixed with the pine of the centerpiece lobby Christmas tree. He shrugged out of his overcoat, scanning the room.

Manetti sat alone near the rear banquette—no jacket. The suntan on his face did not go unnoticed by Rossi amid the winter clothing and colors in the hotel.

Manetti stood and greeted Rossi. They shook hands and sat.

"Appreciate the risk, in meeting", Rossi said, sliding into the booth.

"Risk runs both ways," Manetti answered. "Coffee?"

"Sure, thanks."

Manetti signaled the waitress for two coffees.

Manetti leaned forward, kept his voice low.

"I'm - or was - corporate counsel at Simon & Kershaw. Financial engineering has been my specialty. Over the years, I've helped clients—domestic and foreign—hide billions. It started as 'creative tax planning'; it ended in felony territory. The FBI has been investigating me and the firm for financial crimes. I'm culpable, as is my boss, Christopher Willoughby. I was in the South Tower when the attacks occurred. I got out before they came down. As I was running for my life, I realized this could be the opportunity to escape prosecution and any retribution from clients like Sonny Patrilla. The insurance claim was to cover my tracks, that's all."

Rossi wondered if Manetti thought Willoughby was still alive. And if he told him that he was dead, would he still want to step forward? He decided to keep the information to himself... for now.

"Someone I trusted was killed a couple of months ago," Maretti said, "probably for helping me. A few days ago, me and people close to me were the targets of an assassin. I'm done running."

Rossi studied him. "You're willing to spill the beans on these guys?"

"Yes. In exchange, I'll hand over ledgers, wire transfers, and signing authorities—enough to indict people like Sonny Patrilla and several international actors. I can't go straight to the feds. I need a broker. I'll testify, but not in public and with my identity concealed.

He set a flash drive on the linen. "This is a teaser—bank logs, e-mail chains, signatures. Probable-cause level, nothing more."

Rossi didn't touch it yet. "Why me?"

"Because you're outside the Justice Department politics... and Andrea trusts you. Besides, if Trinity's satisfied that the claim has been withdrawn, you're free to chase bigger game. That's what you've done for all the years as a detective, right?"

Rossi lifted the drive, turning it in his fingers. "So, I help you clear your conscience, maybe the feds put some bad guys in jail, what's in it for me?"

Manetti's eyes hardened. "Satisfaction. But with a big carrot. High-value stolen art. Paintings vanished from European museums, laundered through some very powerful people. I can place them, give shipping dates, manifests, and private vault locations. Bring those home and end your career with a standing ovation."

Rossi exhaled, weighing. "OK, say I can open the door to Assistant U.S. Attorney Justine Gallagher, who runs Organized Crime at the Southern District of New York. She'll meet if I vouch. But no promises on a deal."

"Fair. But I won't surface without a signed proffer. It has to include no public testimony, immunity from past actions taken on behalf of clients, and relocation plans that I approve."

Rossi nodded slowly. "I'll need 48 hours. They'll want confirmation this isn't a stunt, and I need to know I'm not being used."

Manetti tapped the tabletop. "Tell them I'll prove authenticity in person. They'll ask why I'm doing this. The answer is simple: I finally understand what 'victimless' really means. There's more to the story that I'll share if I have a deal. Enough to blow the lid off some very dangerous actors."

Silence sat between them, broken only by *"Have Yourself a Merry Little Christmas"* drifting from hidden speakers throughout the lobby.

Rossi pocketed the drive. "I'll call Gallagher tomorrow. If she bites, I'll e-mail. What's your email address?"

"Send it to Andrea, she'll get it to me."

Manetti stood, offered his hand again. "Thank you, Mr. Rossi. For me and my sister."

"You have an interesting story, for sure. Let's see if it pans out," Rossi said. Then, softer and with a smile, "And call me Rocky—only my boss uses 'Mr.'"

Manetti managed a faint smile. "Michael, then."

They departed into the street under twinkling holiday lights— two men bound by a fragile pact, each wagering his future on the other's word.

CHAPTER 37

THE PITCH

THE departure lounge at Hartsfield-Jackson International hummed with quiet tension. Travelers clutched coffee, stared at phone screens, listened to Walkmans. Rocco Rossi sat near Gate B10, coat draped over his knee, his phone open to a text.

He poked the keys carefully; certain he would never get used to the new technology. Getting too old for this, he thought.

Justine — I know your plate's full. But I've got a credible insider— deep background in shady financial schemes. Tied to racketeering and money laundering, potentially international implications –wants to talk. He wants immunity and protection in exchange for material evidence and an affidavit. You and I both know these don't fall out of the sky every day. Worth a sit-down?

Several minutes passed. Then the reply came:

Nice hearing from you, Rocky. I'm at our St. Andrews Plaza office all week. Can you come in tomorrow at 9 a.m. But I'm not promising anything. And if this is bullshit, you owe me coffee for life.

Rossi smiled faintly. He texted back:

Deal. I'll bring the coffee anyway.

******

The next morning, Rossi arrived ten minutes early at 1 St. Andrews Plaza, the offices of the U.S. Attorney for the Southern District. The Christmas tree in the lobby was enormous, decked in white lights and gold garland. Rossi flashed his credentials. A pair of marshals waved him through security, and he made his way up to the Organized Crime Division.

Justine Gallagher's office door was open. The nameplate read: **Assistant U.S. Attorney – J. Gallagher.** She stood when she saw him, the same blend of cool efficiency and caffeinated fire Rossi remembered from their Trenton days.

She was thirty-eight now, slender, five-six without the four-inch heels that let her meet most men eye-to-eye. Light brown hair with blonde highlights framed a face that balanced courtroom steel with just enough softness to keep juries leaning her way. She favored sharp, tailored suits over flash, but never let anyone forget she was a woman in a world that sometimes mistook competence for coldness.

Gallagher had come up the hard way—Dickinson School of Law, top third academically, but undisputed number one in mock trial, where her cross-examinations could strip a witness to the bone. She was recruited straight out of school to the U.S. Attorney's Trenton branch, starting as a Deputy Attorney General. That was where she and Rossi first crossed paths, back when his badge carried the grime of Trenton's streets and hers the ink of freshly signed indictments.

They'd worked two big cases together. The first was an I-95 human trafficking bust that started with a state trooper taking a bullet on a routine stop and ended with six women—three of them minors—pulled from a van headed for a life they'd never chosen. Rossi had been the lead link between local detectives, state police, and the FBI, developing the intelligence that cracked the ring. Gallagher, as prosecutor, had publicly credited him at a press conference for the takedown.

The second time was bloodier. A mob hit in the Chambersburg section of Trenton—one high-ranking wiseguy gunned down in a crowded Italian restaurant. The feds folded it into an ongoing RICO case, and Gallagher took the lead. Rossi's inside knowledge of Trenton's mob families helped deliver the shooters, and she made sure his contribution was recognized when the arrests were made.

Professionally, they'd been a good match—her surgical precision in court, his bulldog persistence in the field. Personally, there had been no romance, though rumors had followed her in Trenton, whispers about a married state representative. Whether true or not, the gossip and a shifting political climate convinced her she'd hit a ceiling there.

Two years ago, the Southern District of New York poached her, offering more cases, more resources, and the title of Assistant U.S. Attorney. The move eliminated anyof her day-to-day contact with Rossi, but their history was still warm enough to matter.

She smiled quickly now, eyes bright. "Rocco. You're looking well. Good to see you."

He grinned and held up two cups. "One black, one sacrilegiously sugary."

She motioned him in. "Black, thanks," she said with a smile.

The office was stacked with binders and folders, but not chaotic. A whiteboard covered in case code names, dates, and status; a muted

CNN feed on the wall. Behind her desk, the "Glory Wall" displayed certificates, commendations, and framed photographs—Gallagher with two different presidents, with her dogs, and with her late sister's kids. One photo, Rossi knew, was of her niece, the girl she treated like her own daughter.

They sat in the less formal setting of the office, around a glass-topped table and captain's chairs.

"So?" she asked, blowing on the coffee. "Sell me."

Rossi leaned in. "I've got someone who wants to cooperate. Deep financial knowledge. An attorney… at least for now. Worked for a firm under active federal investigation before 9/11. He's spooked; claims there's a target on his back. His material implicates a major crime family—Sonny Patrilla."

Gallagher raised an eyebrow.

"Name certainly rings a bell," she said. "Your guy has reason to be concerned. Patrilla is still a tier 1 target for Justice. We never got Sonny."

"I think this guy can give you Sonny."

She crossed her legs. "Let's slow down. Start from the top. Who is he?"

Rossi shook his head. "He's not giving his name until he has immunity and protection guaranteed. And frankly, I don't blame him."

Gallagher arched an eyebrow. "So, you're asking for a handshake deal. Blindfolded."

"I'm asking for a meeting. And I'm telling you it's worth it."

"Okay. What firm?"

"Simon & Kershaw."

She sat back, surprise flickering across her face.

"That firm got wiped out," she said. "North Tower, I think. That investigation died with them. Willoughby was the focus, right?"

Rossi nodded. "He's the guy. The senior partner who ran the financial division. My firm insured his life. He died in the collapse of the North Tower. Left a wife and two sons."

"And your source worked for him?"

Rossi kept his voice measured. "He did. Close enough to see everything. Offshore entities, shell companies, cash movements, laundering pipelines, the works."

Gallagher frowned. "I remember reading the old files. The problem is, even before the attacks, they kept that stuff airtight. And now, most of the paper is ash, and everyone who could testify is buried under Ground Zero."

Rossi leaned forward. "Not everyone."

She looked at him sharply. "Are you telling me he's one of the Simon & Kershaw lawyers we thought were dead?"

"I didn't say that," Rossi replied. "But yes."

Gallagher blinked. "And he wants to deal."

"He's tired of running. But he's also smart enough not to walk into a courthouse without leverage. He doesn't want a headline. He wants redemption and safety."

She narrowed her eyes. "What's the angle?"

"He's already provided me with a flash drive. Not admissible on its own. But enough to prove he's real. Emails, bank wires, shell companies, fake invoices."

Gallagher sipped her coffee. "So, what does he want?"

"Immunity. Witness protection. A chance to give you what's

left of the old investigation and maybe more. He says he can also tie some of the Patrilla money to local New York real estate development deals. He says the firm laundered through foreign real estate, offshore and European banks, even stolen art."

Gallagher's brow lifted at that. "Art? Huh."

Rossi nodded. "He claims he can identify pieces looted during the Nazi era and other pieces used as currency by organized crime networks."

She let out a long breath.

"That's the kind of thing that lights up INTERPOL. Is this guy real? Sounds like he could blow a few whistles."

"I know how it sounds," Rossi said. "But this guy's not a con. He could've disappeared forever. Instead, he reached out—through me, through his sister."

She studied him. "You trust him?"

"I do. He's scared. He's flawed. But he wants to set things right. This isn't about cash or fame. This is a man who watched the Towers fall around him…. maybe he suddenly got religion."

A long pause.

Gallagher stood, walked to the window, and looked out over the city.

"My office," she said slowly, "has six open cases involving foreign terrorists, eleven RICO (Racketeer Influenced and Corrupt Organizations Act) cases, and five active mob crews under investigation. Half my team is working 60-hour weeks. I don't have the manpower to chase ghosts."

Rossi rose too. "He's not a ghost. He's probably your best shot in years to take down Sonny Patrilla and maybe some other bad actors."

She turned. "You say he wants redemption. Is he willing to testify?"

"If the deal's right, yes."

"He'll need to sign a proffer. Swear to everything."

Rossi nodded. "He knows that."

Gallagher chewed the inside of her cheek. "Let me be clear: we can't offer a blanket deal without knowing the full scope. But I'll take the flash drive. I'll vet it. If it checks out, he gets a preliminary interview. No promises beyond that."

Rossi stepped forward and placed the flash drive on her desk. "That's all I'm asking."

Gallagher picked it up gently.

"He's lucky you're the one who found him," she said.

Rossi shrugged. "Luck had nothing to do with it. He was smart enough to reach out. And he's desperate enough to do something meaningful."

She nodded. "Alright, Rocco. Let me do my due diligence. If it's real, you'll hear from me."

Rossi offered his hand. "Thanks, Justine. I know you didn't have to take this meeting."

She shook it. "We go way back. I owed you that much."

That afternoon, Rossi sat at his desk in Brooklyn, the late December sky gunmetal gray. He opened a fresh message in the Lazarus draft folder.

Andrea —

Please let Michael know I've done what I could. Gallagher isn't ready to move forward. Too much backlog, not enough resources.

She didn't say no. But she didn't say yes.

I'll stay in touch. Tell him to be careful. We may need more raw evidence to push her over the edge.

—*Rocco Rossi.*

He leaned back in his chair, looked toward the window, and thought, what else does Manetti have? Does he have more leverage?

The next move is up to Justine Gallagher.

CHAPTER 38

THE UNMASKING

THE Wharf Motel was quiet in the mid-morning hush, seagulls squawking overhead as Emily Foster stepped lightly onto the weathered porch. The salt air mingled with the scent of diesel drifting in from the shrimp docks. She wore jeans and a navy R.E.E.F. T-shirt—casual, unassuming. The key Dean had left for her in a white envelope at the front desk was in her pocket.

He'd told her it was fine to stop by, that he'd be in Miami for a few days handling something "complicated." She'd left her diving watch on the nightstand and needed it for a reef survey that afternoon.

She hadn't planned to do anything more than grab the watch and go. But that was before the shotgun attack. Before the speedboat, the gunfire, and the fear in Dean's voice when he told her he thought he was the target.

Now she wasn't so sure about anything but knew she needed answers.

Inside room six, the scents were faint but familiar—soap on the sink, and him. The bed was made. His duffel bag sat neatly in the corner, zipped shut. The small table held an empty glass and a folded copy of the *USA Today* dated two days earlier. His toothbrush in the cup by the sink.

Nothing screamed danger. No gun under the pillow.

Still, she moved with hesitation. This was his space. His privacy. But he had opened the door. He had told her to go in.

And yet… since the attack on the *Kitty Jo*, something had shifted. He'd grown quieter, guarded. The relaxed ease between them had tightened. She told herself she wasn't snooping—she just needed clarity. Something to explain what kind of man finds himself chased down by men with guns.

She crossed the room. Bent to retrieve the watch she spotted on the floor beside the nightstand.

That should've been it.

But as she turned to leave, she noticed something half-tucked beneath a towel on the desk chair. A corner of a manila envelope. Ordinary. Forgettable. But it was out of place. From what little she knew of Dean, he was neat, meticulous, with everything in its place.

Curiosity crept in. Not reckless, not panicked. Just… cautious. She lifted the towel.

One glance at the label and her stomach flipped.

Michael Manetti — General Delivery, Key West, FL 33040

Her breath caught in her throat. She stared at it for a beat too long, pulses suddenly in her ears. The name meant nothing to her—yet the shock of seeing it in Dean's room made it mean everything.

She opened the unsealed envelope. Slowly. Carefully. Inside were letters and legal documents. Several pages on the letterhead of Simon & Kershaw LLP. One signed "Michael A. Manetti, Esq."

Others referenced offshore accounts, wire transfers, and a man named Christopher Willoughby.

The hair stood up on her arms.

She set the envelope on the desk, fingers trembling. Sat down on the edge of the bed, heart pounding hard against her ribs.

Dean Broussard—if that was even his real name—wasn't just some burned-out finance guy looking for a fresh start. He could be someone else. Someone with a past buried under layers of paper.

Someone dangerous?

She didn't know. Not yet.

But she would find out.

Her stomach churned. The man she'd kissed, slept beside, and fallen in love with—may have lied to her about who he was. And, she was now wondering, had everything been a lie?

She left the motel confused and with a million questions. The envelope was still inside the room. But the trust she had carried was gone. If her suspicions proved true, she would demand answers.

******

That evening, as Manetti's plane returned from Atlanta and touched down in Key West, he sent her a text:

"Home. Dinner? Carmella's at 7?"

Emily took ten minutes to respond.

"Let's do K.C. Steakhouse. Busier."

He raised an eyebrow when he read it. K.C.'s? Busier wasn't like her.

At 6:50 p.m., Manetti walked into the K.C. Steakhouse on Caroline Street. The place was packed, lively, the bar area loud with happy-hour energy. He spotted her in a corner booth, already seated.

She looked beautiful, but distant.

"Hey," he said, walking over to kiss her, then hesitating.

She didn't smile. "Hi."

He slid onto the bench seat across the table from her. "I thought you hated chain steakhouses."

She lifted her iced tea. "Felt like a change."

They exchanged pleasantries, the weather, and the reef restoration project. But Emily's tone was off. She wasn't teasing him like usual. Her warmth had a glaze over it.

"How was Miami?" she asked suddenly.

"Busy. Wrapped up some paperwork, banking stuff. Trying to extend my stay here," he said. "What about your dad? Is he still working on repairs to the *Kitty Jo*?"

She tilted her head. "Nice deflection."

He blinked. "What?"

"I stopped by the motel to pick up my watch," she said quietly. "Who is Michael Manetti? I saw the envelope."

His eyes lifted. Emily's face was unreadable.

Silence. His mouth opened, but nothing came out for a moment.

Then: "Emily, I was going to tell you."

"When?"

"I was waiting for the right time—"

"There's never a right time to find out the man I've been seeing has lied about his name, his life, his past. What else have you lied about?" she said angrily.

He looked stricken. "Not about how I feel about you."

Her voice cracked. "Then why didn't you trust me?"

Manetti looked down at the table. He took a breath and lifted his eyes.

"It's true, I'm Michael Manetti," he said finally in a low voice. "I was an attorney at Simon & Kershaw in New York. I worked in their financial practice. We catered to… high-risk clients. Some criminal, some foreign, all rich. I helped set up shell companies, hid assets, and laundered money. I didn't ask too many questions. Told myself it was just business."

"And 9/11, and why you're here in Key West?" she asked curtly.

"I was in the Towers when they were hit, meeting an old friend and business colleague. He informed me that he was interviewed by two FBI agents the Friday before regarding clients he and I shared. While we were having coffee, my office called to tell me two Special Agents were asking for me. I knew it would be trouble. I know too much. I have some dangerous, powerful clients who would rather see me dead than talk to the FBI. I not only feared prison, but I feared for my life if certain people thought I was a danger to them."

Emily's eyes widened as Manetti's mysterious past unfolded before her eyes.

"Ralph, that was my friend who I met that morning. He and I heard on the TV in the coffee shop that the North Tower was hit, then all hell broke out on the concourse level where we were meeting. I made it out as the first debris began to fall. I never saw Ralph again. Weeks later, his name was listed among the dead. That was devastating to me. We knew each other our entire lives. In the chaos, no one I know saw me leave. I saw a way out—a way to disappear. I took it. At first, I just wanted time. Space to figure things out. Then, an old friend of my father in New Orleans helped me build a new identity. And then… I met you."

Emily's eyes glistened. "And this has all been fake? Your job at the bank… us?"

"No. Nothing between us was fake. You… you've been the one real thing in a long time, even beyond all that came before."

Emily shook her head. "But you lied to me. You let me open my heart to someone who doesn't exist."

He leaned forward. "I didn't plan to fall in love with you. But I did. And I can't hide this from you anymore."

She looked at him, raw and torn. "I need time. I don't know if I can believe anything you say."

She stood abruptly. "I need air."

And she walked out.

******

The Foster house was quiet when Manetti knocked early the next evening. Jim answered, eyes narrowing.

"Evening, Jim," Manetti said.

Jim stepped aside. "You here to explain yourself?"

"Yes. All of it."

Emily sat curled on the couch, arms crossed. Her cheeks were flushed.

Manetti stood in the middle of the room. "Mr. Foster. Emily. I owe you both everything. And an apology."

He then sat across from them, turning to address Jim. "Jim, my real name is Michael Manetti. I used to be a partner attorney at Simon & Kershaw in Manhattan. It was located on two floors of the North Tower of the World Trade Center. I worked under a senior partner named Christopher Willoughby. Our department helped clients obscure their assets from the law, creditors, unfriendly governments, and sometimes, spouses—tax shelters, offshore accounts, and I'm certain…stolen art. You name it."

He paused, steadying his breath.

"I never asked too many questions. It was lucrative. I was caught up in it. Then 9/11 happened. I was on the concourse level of the South Tower. I survived, but no one knew. I've been presumed dead. My office was below the impact zone on the 76th floor of the North Tower. My administrative assistant knew I was out of the building in a meeting. She didn't survive. When the building came down, everyone assumed I'd died too."

Jim leaned forward. "So, you vanished."

"Yes. With help, I became Dean Broussard. But I wasn't hiding so much from prosecution—I was hiding from my clients. From the Patrilla family, for one, a New York crime family. I handled some of their financial affairs. With an FBI investigation underway, I feared they would think I had flipped. When I narrowly escaped the collapse, I realized it was an opportunity to disappear, to take time to think, and to come up with a plan.

"And then I met you two. That day on the charter with you," motioning toward Jim, "I started to realize a different life. Along the way, I fell in love with your daughter and found meaning again and hope for a future."

Emily spoke, her voice quiet. "You said there's more. That someone helped you and got killed?"

"Sailor. An Army friend of my father. He was murdered. He was my connection in New Orleans. He provided me with fake identification in case I found it necessary to leave the country. I think the Patrilla family tracked him down and killed him. Then the attack on the *Kitty Jo*—it wasn't random. I think Sonny Patrilla found Sailor and tracked me here. I've got evidence against him. I could testify and expose records, names, and transactions. Enough to put him away. Maybe others, too."

Jim sat back, jaw tight.

Turning to address Emily, "I met with an investigator, Rocco Rossi. A former cop. We met in Atlanta, not Miami. I thought the Atlanta hub could conceal me from Florida. He works for the insurance company that insured my life. Earlier, I asked my sister, Andrea, to put a claim in. She's the beneficiary of my policy. I thought that would help my disappearance. But somehow Rossi became suspicious, and Andrea became afraid. He convinced her that he suspected I was alive and in trouble, that he could help me. He's taking what I gave him to the U.S. Attorney. I'm offering to testify. But I need protection. Immunity. Maybe witness relocation.

"Since you have brought me into your lives, I owe you both the truth. Because it affects you. And because I love you, Emily. I didn't know how to tell you. I thought I was protecting you. But I see now I was wrong."

Silence fell.

Jim looked at his daughter.

Pause.

"There's more to the story", Manetti continued. "One of the firm's clients is a Saudi businessman by the name of Ziad Abdullah. He is very wealthy and powerful in the Middle East. He has Saudi royal connections." Manetti paused. "I have evidence that ties him to the attack on the World Trade Center."

"Oh my God!" Emily exclaimed.

With raw emotions, Jim jumped from his seat, yelling, "What the hell have you been involved with?"

"I know, it's incredible. I had no idea of any ties Abdullah had with terrorists. Abdullah came to our office for a meeting with my colleague Christopher Willoughby. Willoughby said Abdullah had an interest in helping a Saudi student get settled in the U.S. and asked me to put together some funds from Abdullah's accounts. A total of $500,000. It certainly was a lot of money, but for the clients I dealt with, this was not an unusual amount. I had no idea, and I don't think Willoughby had any idea what it was all about. Then, just weeks ago, I saw the so-called student's face on TV. He was the hijacker pilot who flew into the Pentagon. His name was Hani Hanjour."

The room went silent.

A few moments later, Emily turned to Manetti. "I can't believe this. You knew this, all this time."

"I've been silent too long. The knowledge I have of Abdullah, the attack on us, the murder of Sailor, and how I began to see a new life with you has changed everything. That's why I met with the investigator. I now see a path forward.

"I trust you. I need people I believe in. I need you to try to trust me. And, because hiding isn't living, I'm done with that. Until recently, I viewed my work for these people as victimless crimes. But now, with the lives lost on September 11th...." Manetti hesitated. Choked up with tears in his eyes, he continued, "I see there are no victimless crimes. Lots of people, innocent people, can be impacted."

Jim rubbed his jaw, turned to Emily, then stood and said, "This is all too much to absorb now. I need to think about all this."

Emily looked at Manetti. Her eyes were still filled with hurt. But something else flickered there now—hope.

"Don't lie to me again," she said.

"I won't," Manetti replied. "I'll answer all your questions."

CHAPTER 39

BUREAUCRATIC GRAVITY

JUSTINE Gallagher stood at the window of her office in the St. Andrews Plaza, her gaze fixed on the grey swirl of traffic crawling along the streets below. Snow was threatening again. A weather advisory blinked across the lower right corner of her monitor. She hated winter in Manhattan—icy sidewalks, canyon winds, cold coffee.

Behind her, the door opened without a knock. It was Nathan Park, her Deputy Chief for Investigations.

"Rocco Rossi's flash drive," he said, holding up a sealed evidence bag. "I've had IT forensics on it already."

Gallagher turned. "Thanks. What's your read?"

Park shrugged. "Says it's from a financial insider. Metadata looks credible. Files are surprisingly well organized. Names match up with old Simon & Kershaw wire-room documents that we flagged pre-9/11. There's a Patrilla trail here, but I haven't found a direct smoking gun yet. No financial routing we can use to subpoena a bank. Not yet."

"Anything on the foreign clients?"

"Shell companies, nominee directors, offshore banks—standard fare. Could tie into broader money laundering, maybe some international cooperation plays. But no obvious Foreign Account Tax Compliance Act (FATCA) violations or Suspicious Activity Report (SAR) triggers we didn't already suspect. It's intriguing bait right now, but..."

"It's a gamble," Gallagher finished.

Park nodded. "Appears to be."

Gallagher turned to her conference table, already laid out with printed excerpts from the flash drive: wire confirmations, scanned client letters, a few flagged email strings. She leafed through the one labeled *"S&K-PATRILLA-CORRESP-2001."*

"Christopher Willoughby's signature," she murmured, pointing. "He was a known associate. Killed in the North Tower. If our guy worked under him, he might be credible."

Park folded his arms. "Still doesn't change that we've got zero access to the original investigation files. And their leads dried up when the building came down. There's no active case to latch this onto."

"Yet," she said.

He nodded, unconvinced. "Right. Yet."

Just then, Ava Ramirez, the office's senior financial crimes analyst, entered. She slid into a chair beside the whiteboard.

"I scrubbed that transaction series he labeled *Amber Key Holdings,*" she said, clicking open her laptop. "All digital trails are less than two hops from Simon & Kershaw's corporate account. That's not something you see in clean money. If I had to guess, this Manetti guy was setting up fake holding companies—"

Gallagher's eyes narrowed. "Wait, Manetti?"

Ramirez glanced up. "That's the name on the email headers embedded in the PDFs. Michael Manetti. Does that ring?"

Park looked to Gallagher, who kept her expression neutral.

"We had someone under that name on a missing persons list from the Towers," Park offered carefully. "Presumed dead. He was an associate at S&K, supposedly."

Gallagher's jaw tensed. "Supposedly. Until now."

The room went still.

"If this is Manetti," she said, "and he's resurfaced with this data. What's his angle? Maybe Rossi is right. He wants redemption."

"But also," Park added, "he may have evidence to bring down a crime family."

"Or he's just trying to save his skin," Ramirez said, crossing her arms. "If he wants a deal, he needs to ante up. Not vague trails."

Gallagher nodded. "Agreed. We can't run a full-court press on speculation and reconstructed ledgers. The standard's higher now. We'd need corroboration, fresh wire activity, maybe an active RICO angle. Right now, we've got little to work on."

She paced slowly. "Okay. Let's say he's legit. Let's say this is Michael Manetti, and he's got the goods. What does he need to do for us to take the meeting?"

Ramirez listed off on her fingers. "Full proffer in writing. First-hand, credible, and actionable information. Corroborating evidence and testimony."

Gallagher scribbled notes. "What about protective custody?"

Park answered, "We can recommend it, but without a charging document or sealed indictment, Witness Security won't even look at the paperwork."

She gave a wry smile. "So, Manetti basically could be walking into a poker game with few chips."

"Unless he creates a public stir with credible information," Ramirez said.

Gallagher looked up.

"You mean—what?"

Ramirez smirked. "People like Manetti don't wait long. If he's desperate, he'll try to force your hand. Media leak, SEC tip, anonymous drop to a whistleblower org. You'll hear about him again, Justine. Just maybe not first."

Gallagher stood straight and ran her hand through her dark hair.

"Thanks, both of you. I'll make the call."

******

Rocco Rossi sat in his Trenton apartment, laptop open, catching up on open claims and resolving older ones when his phone buzzed.

Justine Gallagher's name appeared on caller ID.

He answered immediately.

"Rossi," he said, trying to sound optimistic.

"Hi, Rocco," Gallagher said. "You got a minute?"

"Always."

He stood, the phone to his ear, pacing between his kitchenette and the TV stand.

"I've reviewed the data," Gallagher said. "You were right—there's enough there to start a conversation. But that's all it is for now. A conversation."

"So you're moving forward?"

"Not yet. There's no foundation we can build on at the moment. What he provided is a tease. Nothing actionable, but he's established threads that are credible. The Simon & Kershaw investigation was effectively buried when the towers fell. Willoughby's dead. The other partners, too. The FBI lost its team and its files. This Manetti— if that's his real name—is coming in naked."

"How did you get his name?" Rossi asked, confused.

"One of my staff caught it in an email heading", Gallagher answered.

A pause.

"I'm sympathetic, Rocco," she said finally. "I know what people went through that day. But this office isn't a confessional booth. If your guy wants immunity, we need more."

"What would that look like?" he asked.

Gallagher's tone stayed firm. "He needs to prove criminal activity. We need documents and names we can subpoena. We need him to corroborate and testify. Without that, and with everything else my department is dealing with, we're not wasting time."

Rossi sighed. "So, where do we go from here?"

"The door's open. But he needs to knock harder."

Rossi nodded, even though she couldn't see him.

"I'll pass it along," he said. "Thanks for listening."

"And Rocco," she added, her voice softening, "if he's really in danger, tell him to be careful. These people don't forget."

Rossi hung up and sat back on the couch, exhaling slowly.

******

Later that night, in his low-lit room at The Wharf Motel, Michael Manetti sat at the small desk. He opened the Lazarus email account. The reply from Rossi via Andrea blinked on the screen.

No offer yet. They won't move unless we give them more. New leverage. They know it's Michael. His name showed up in an email header. Be careful. What more does he have? Rocco Rossi

Manetti stared at it for a full minute, fingers hovering above the keyboard.

Realizing his identity was exposed, he had to move fast now to make a deal.

Without responding, he closed the file, opened a blank document page, and slowly began to type—not a reply to Rossi, but a script for something else entirely.

A trap.

If they wanted proof that the Patrilla family was still laundering money, he'd give them a transaction they couldn't ignore.

Manetti reached for the leather folder beside him. Inside was the transaction model, *Starling & Co. Advisory,* that he would use to expose Patrilla.

Releasing proof of a direct link to Patrilla could send a shockwave. It would be bold; it would be indisputable—and it would be dangerous.

It would get Gallagher's attention, but also Sonny Patrilla's.

He began to type an outline for a transaction.

CHAPTER 40

TIDES OF TRUTH

THE day after his frustrating update from Rossi, Manetti stood outside the R.E.E.F. headquarters in Old Town, hands in the pockets of his windbreaker, squinting against the late morning sun. The Gulf shimmered beyond the marina's edge, a gentle breeze rattled the palms. Through the window, he could see Emily inside, hunched over a desktop, sorting through folders.

He hadn't slept much. Rossi's message about the Assistant U.S. Attorney left him feeling like he was stuck in legal purgatory—too guilty to be clear, too valuable to get rid of, but still no deal. The sting of rejection from Emily hadn't gone away either. But he was ready to fix what he could. Starting now.

He went to the R.E.E.F. office just to see her face. Not wanting to face her at work, he walked to a pay phone and dialed the office landline. After two rings, her voice came on.

"R.E.E.F., Emily Foster speaking."

"Hey," Manetti said, trying to sound casual, but it came out heavy.

There was a pause. "Dean?"

"No," he corrected gently. "It's Michael. It's time I stopped hiding from the name."

Another beat of silence.

"What do you want?" she asked flatly.

I'd like to talk with you and your dad. I have a plan to make everything right…for me…and you. It's risky, but it's the best shot I have to expose Patrilla and Abdullah, to end this for good.

"Are you asking for help?" she said, guarded but curious.

"I'm asking for a chance…for us. And yes, I'd like your help. Both of you. Can we meet at the charter office later today?"

She didn't answer right away. Then: "Three o'clock."

"I'll be there."

******

Manetti arrived early. The air inside the small charter shack smelled like old bait and weathered wood. The framed fishing photos along the wall seemed frozen in time—smiles, sunshine, trophy catches raised in triumph. He couldn't help but notice the picture of Emily at fifteen, holding a marlin almost as tall as she was, eyes bright and determined. She had always known her mind. That's what he loved—and feared.

Emily and Jim arrived together from the dock just after three. Jim's jaw was tight. Emily looked like she hadn't slept either.

She crossed her arms as she stood in front of him. "You said you wanted to explain. So, explain."

Manetti stood. "Emily, Jim. I owe you both more than apologies. But I'll start there. I lied. I let you believe I was someone I wasn't because I wanted a new life so badly—one with peace, with someone who didn't know my past. That wasn't fair to either of you."

Jim folded his arms across his chest. "You're damn right it wasn't."

Manetti nodded, taking the hit. "I understand your anger. I do. But I didn't come here to defend what I did. I came because I'm done running. I want to finish this."

He turned to Emily, his voice softening. "And I want to be honest—with you—completely. I've fallen in love with you, Emily. The person who stood beside me when we fought off a speedboat attack in open water. Who confronted me when she learned the truth. You're fearless, brilliant, and... I want to be worthy of you."

Emily's eyes glistened, but she held his gaze.

"I don't know how to process what I found in your motel room," she said. "That envelope—those documents. It was like watching someone I love turn into a stranger right in front of me."

Manetti's throat tightened. "I know."

"You let me think I knew you. You let me fall in love with someone who didn't exist."

"I didn't expect to fall in love," said Manetti. "And when I did, I was already too deep in the lie. I wanted to protect you. I still do."

Her arms dropped to her sides, shoulders tense.

"Don't ever do that again," she said, voice trembling. "Don't ever decide what I can or can't handle. You don't get to lie and say it was for my safety."

"I won't," Manetti said. "No more secrets."

She took a deep breath, brushing a strand of hair behind her ear. "You want my help?"

"Yes."

"Then tell us the plan."

They sat around the chart table, with the scent of the afternoon low tide drifting through the open windows. Manetti pulled out a notepad.

"The investigator, Rossi, met with the U.S. Attorney. She's interested but won't move forward unless I can give them a live transaction—real money laundering activity that proves the Patrilla network is still operating. Without that, I'm just another dead-end witness with no leverage."

Jim leaned forward. "So, what's your play?"

"I still have access to accounts—one that has been used by Patrilla's network. There's an opening. I can trigger a real transaction from that account to one in New York, linked to a shell company controlled by Patrilla. It'll be flagged by any serious anti-money laundering protocols.

The second part of the plan is to expose Ziad Abdullah. I have access to one of his accounts that holds a prince's fortune. That will come into play, too, along with releasing documentation included in the envelope Emily found in my room. Solid evidence of Abdullah's involvement in funding Hanjour.

Emily frowned. "How can you do that without getting caught?"

I need to visit the bank and meet my contact there in person. That's why I have to get to Bimini. But I can't go through immigration—it's too risky now that they know I'm alive. I'd also like to save my new passport for leaving the country if necessary. I'm unsure how good the forgery is, so I can't be certain I'd get back into the U.S. safely.

Jim nodded slowly. "You want to do this off the books. No

paper trail."

"Exactly. I'd need someone to take me. Someone I can trust. Someone who knows those waters."

Jim sat back. "So that's where we come in."

Manetti hesitated. "Yes. I know I'm asking a lot."

"I wouldn't do this for you," Jim said. "I'd do it for my daughter, if that's what she wants."

"I understand."

Emily looked at him. "Who's the contact in Bimini?"

"Emil Dubois. He's the bank manager. I've worked with him for years. He's discreet and knows what I've been doing—but not loyal to anyone. If I offer the right incentive, I think he'll help facilitate the transactions."

Jim exhaled through his nose. "Sounds like a hell of a gamble."

"It is," Manetti said. "But if it works, it could take down the Patrilla crime family and link Abdullah to the terror attack. From there, the authorities will get leads to others involved in organizing it. And it keeps me valuable to the Justice Department—maybe enough for them to offer immunity."

There was silence in the room as waves outside lapped against the docks.

Jim stood and walked to the window. He stared out toward the marina, toward the *Kitty Jo*.

"You know what hurts the most?" he confessed. "That I let you into my home. I saw you as a man with a story not ready to be disclosed. Maybe a little too private, but decent. Then you risked my daughter's life. That speedboat wasn't just some coincidence. They were coming for you. And she was caught in the middle."

Manetti's chest tightened. "I'll never forgive myself for that. But I can promise you this: I will never put her in harm's way again. I'll risk everything to make that true."

Emily walked to her father and put her hand on his arm.

"Dad," she said quietly. "I believe him."

Jim looked at her, his expression a blend of concern and resignation.

"I don't trust him yet," he said. "But I trust you."

He turned to Manetti. "You've got one shot. You cross a line—any line—I pull the plug."

"Fair."

Jim nodded. "The weather looks favorable for the next few days. We could leave tomorrow. The *Kitty Jo*'s fueled and ready, are you?"

"Yes, sir. I can finish up details on the way over."

Emily walked back to Manetti. Her voice was softer now.

"Don't screw this up," she said. "Because I do love you. That hasn't changed. But if I catch you lying to me again—about anything—it's over."

Manetti stepped closer, his hand brushing hers.

"No more lies," he said. "Not ever."

She nodded, swallowing the emotion welling behind her eyes. "Then we'll do this. Together."

******

Later that night, Manetti stood outside the motel, watching the stars scatter across the sky. Emily came from the road, crossing the parking lot, jacket zipped against the wind.

"I left some notes for work," she said. "They'll be covered while we're gone."

He smiled. "Thank you."

She studied his face. "This thing in Bimini—if we're really doing it, I need to know one thing."

"Anything."

"Is this just about justice, or is this your way of trying to erase the past?"

Manetti considered it.

"Maybe both," he said. "But I want a future more than I want a clean slate. And that future, if I'm lucky, includes you."

She stepped close, her forehead resting against him.

"Then let's get this done."

They stood in silence for a long moment. The tide turned slowly beneath them, and nearby, the *Kitty Jo* bobbed in her slip, waiting for morning.

Together, they would chart a new course.

CHAPTER 41

TO BIMINI BEFORE DARK

Kitty Jo's long, solid hull ran smooth.

J IM Foster turned the bow east through Boca Chica Channel. Lights from the Naval Air Station winked, then disappeared. The sea opened wide before them. The rising sun appeared over the horizon, changing color from orange to yellow to blinding. Emily brewed coffee in the galley.

"Six hours to Miami," Jim said.

They refueled in Miami. No questions there. Manetti paid cash. The female attendant waved goodbye from the fuel dock. No paperwork.

At dusk, they crossed the eighty miles into Bahamian waters and the Sweet Water Creek outside of Alice Town, Bimini, running lights off. Clarence was waiting.

Jim cut the engine. Emily leaned out, saw the man wave from the dock.

"Good to see you, Jim," Clarence yelled out across the creek.

"Long time," Jim responded.

"Where do you want her?"

"Back dock," Jim said.

Clarence nodded. No questions. He owed Jim. Navy stuff, long past.

They tied up behind the tin-roofed shack. Clarence's eyes locked on Emily, handling the lines in a two-piece bathing suit. "Is that the same girl you brought around the base? Damn near a kid back then."

"Emily, say hi."

She smiled politely. Eyes cool to Clarence's leer. She quickly excused herself to the task.

"She's sharp and good-looking, like her mother," Clarence said.

"She is."

The *Kitty Jo* was secured and out of sight from the creek. Inside the dock shack, Jim and Clarence had cold beer.

"She's got business in town tomorrow with Dean. We may be a few days. We won't make trouble for you."

Clarence grinned. "Then, while they're working, let's fish."

"It's a deal", Jim answered.

They clinked bottles and said no more.

******

It rained in the afternoon. A humid, steady rain that glossed the decks of the *Kitty Jo* without cooling the air. The kind of rain that just added weight to the heat.

Manetti hunched over the table in the main cabin, tapping at his laptop. The fan wheezed in the corner. Emily poured two cups of warm coffee and leaned over his shoulder.

The glow of green on his laptop screen lit their faces.

"This one," Manetti said, tapping the touchpad, "was for Patrilla."

Emily squinted. The filename read: *NassauCove_Consult_SA.docx*

"Shell company," he explained. "Based in the Bahamas. Supposedly, coastal infrastructure consulting. In reality? Funded by money flowing through a strip club in Atlantic City. Just a P.O. box, and a Nassau lawyer paid three hundred bucks a month to sign forms and keep his mouth shut."

He clicked again.

"This invoice here. Seventy-eight grand. Labeled 'Strategic Marine Infrastructure Reports.' Sent from Nassau to another shell in Panama."

Emily crossed her arms. "And the Panama company?"

"They held a U.S. bank account in Miami: Petros Global. It paid the invoice without blinking."

She frowned. "So... strip club money in Jersey ends up in the Bahamas through a bunch of fake companies?"

He nodded. "Cash from the club gets broken up across fake businesses, wired to Panama, then to Nassau. On paper, it's all looks legit."

Emily sat across from him, brow furrowed. "And who owns the top shell?"

"An anonymous trust in Gibraltar. That's where the trail goes dark."

"Jesus," she whispered rhetorically, "How deep does this go?"

He clicked open another folder: *QatariTrade_Link1999*

"This one's worse," he said. "Ziad Abdullah. Three wires total $2.3 million. Marked for 'rare earth metals.' Supposedly headed to China."

"Were there any metals?"

"Technically, yes. But not this shipment. It was ghost cargo. My guy in Singapore faked the manifests. The customs docs. Everything."

Emily studied the spreadsheet.

"So, this is your leverage," she said.

Manetti sipped his coffee, grimacing. "Insurance. I knew I could be a fall guy one day if the FBI came knocking. So, I saved the patterns. Not crimes on their own, but enough to unravel the whole mess."

She looked at him. "And the art part?"

He hesitated. "Later. That's even messier."

He clicked open another file. A flowchart lit up the screen: circles, arrows, names.

"This is where it gets loud," he said. A shell firm in Isle of Man submitted two identical invoices by mistake. Same amount, same date, different recipients. Someone got lazy."

Emily leaned in. "Why does that matter?"

"Noise attracts audits. A duplicate invoice means something doesn't line up. The bank freezes the account. Investigators start tracing ownership. It snowballs."

He looked up at her. "I'll use this model on Patrilla. I plan to make noise. Enough to draw in the Justice Department."

Manetti turned back to the computer and clicked open one last folder *Collateral_Selloff/April*

"Dubai deal. Dirty cash. Funneled through a Paris art house. The problem was that the art was stolen from Denmark. Twenty years ago."

Emily blinked. "Where was it?"

"An Italian freeport."

"Freeport?" she asked. "That sounds like a Bond villain hideout."

Manetti smiled. "Not far off. Think of a freeport as a high-security, tax-free warehouse. Good intentions by governments to promote international trade, but like other good intentions, they turned to illicit activities. Goods—especially art—can sit there indefinitely. No customs. No taxes. It stays off the books."

"That sounds like a loophole."

"It's a loophole the wealthy and corrupt use to hide assets. Paintings, ancient artifacts become just collateral. Sometimes the art never leaves its crate or the freeport facility, even when resold or traded."

Emily shook her head. "I've read about stolen art from museums but had no idea how criminals could use it like that."

He looked at her, his expression heavy.

"I built this machine to be untouchable," he said. "Now I'm going to use it to burn them down."

She reached across the table, her hand finding his.

"You're really going to do it?"

"Yeah." He shut the laptop. The rain eased outside.

"First, the Sonny Patrilla, to get the Feds' attention. Then I'll pull on some very expensive Saudi threads."

Emily sat back. Her voice was quiet.

"And when their schemes start to fall apart?"

Manetti stood. A mild wake slowly rocked the boat.

"That's when I stop running," he said. "And start living again."

CHAPTER 42

LEDGERS AND LIES

Tuesday, December 18th

JACOB, a local boy, had a golf cart. He wore flip-flops and a Yankees cap.

"Need a ride, mahn?"

For $5 U.S., he would drive them to town.

Manetti nodded. He and Emily hopped on.

Emily sat beside him, quiet. The cart buzzed over a sand-pitted path toward the two-lane King's Road leading to Alice Town, the commercial center of the 9 square miles of islands.

Bimini smelled of salt, cooking oil, and fish under the subtropical sun. Boats lined the shore; small ones, painted bright in reds, yellows, and turquoise. Kids played with dogs. Men gutted fish with bloodied knives.

Colorful, rusted tin-roofed shacks leaned toward the turquoise sea. Shop signs, hand-painted, promoting crafts and souvenirs. The place bore scars. It was authentic.

"End of the World Saloon," Jacob said, pointing toward the beach bar as they drove by. "Good conch, mahn."

They passed the bar with the sound of his horn and a wave from the bartender recognizing Jacob. Music played. Reggae, or something close. People laughed and waved to the passersby. A drunken man, staggering back and forth, sang to no one in particular.

At the central plaza, Manetti and Emily got out. Manetti handed Jacob a five.

"Appreciate it, mahn."

******

The heat came early. Dry on the skin, then wet as the humidity increased. The wind was slow, the sea flat.

Emily and Manetti strolled through Alice Town before the shops opened. The street was empty except for dogs and a barefoot boy dragging a stick through the dust. Chickens scuttled from under carts.

Emily wore sunglasses and a wide straw hat. Manetti carried a canvas satchel.

The bank was on the south corner of the shaded square. White walls. Closed windows. A/C humming. A brass plaque on the wall read: *Société Française Suisse Banque.*

Inside was Emil Dubois, branch manager. French Swiss heritage. Thick glasses. Exiled to the tropics for something he denied doing.

He once told Manetti, drunk, about a scandal back home in Switzerland. Not his fault, he said. But they sent him here.

He made peace with paradise, living comfortably by the sea with his wife and daughter.

Manetti remembered that night.

Dubois was vulnerable.

They climbed the three stone steps shortly after the doors were unlocked. Inside, it was cool and quiet. The air smelled faintly of fresh-cut flowers. The office staff, mainly Bahamian, was attractive and friendly.

Dubois met Manetti and Emily in the lobby. His shirt was crisp, covered by a tan tropical linen suit. No tie. He wore a watch that cost too much.

"You're early," he said.

"Nice to see you again, Emil," Manetti replied.

Manetti introduced Emil, "My compatriot, Emily", purposely omitting her surname.

Dubois turned to Emily, nodding with slow, old-world charm.

"Enchanté, mademoiselle," he said, taking her hand. "This way, please," spoken in English with a French accent.

They passed empty desks. A fan clicked in the corner. The walls were plain except for a faded print of a glacier in Montreux and a map of the Caribbean.

Clients came to the bank not for décor, but for discretion.

Dubois led them into a small room with louvered shutters cracked open allowing in the cool morning breeze. The ocean was visible between buildings. An empty cargo boat returning to Miami moved slowly headed toward the south reef.

He and Emily sat at the conference table. Manetti stayed standing.

"I brought the account files we talked about on the phone. Bank info, login credentials, everything we need," Manetti said.

Emily watched quietly. Watched Dubois. Watched Manetti. Listening and learning.

Manetti opened the envelope and spread the folders on the

desk like cards.

"A few days ago, Emil, someone tried to kill Emily and me... and her father," he said. "And a man I trusted—an old family friend who helped me—was murdered in New Orleans a few weeks earlier".

He turned toward Emily.

"I believe Sonny Patrilla ordered all of it."

Dubois took off his glasses. "The same Sonny, your client, no?"

Manetti nodded. "My firm and I were being investigated for work we did for him. I'm supposed to be dead from the attack on the World Trade Center. I think he's making sure that becomes true."

"Why now?" Dubois asked.

"Because I know too much. And I'm a loose end."

Dubois leaned back. "You want revenge, eh?"

"No," Manetti said. "Maybe retribution... and redemption. They tried to kill me and someone I love. I'm done helping men like Patrilla bury money as they bury bodies."

He handed Dubois the binder. "These are what I'm calling the Canary Ledgers. They document the laundering operations. I'll create transactions based on their old patterns—patterns you and I have used before—similar enough to pass first inspection. But unlike the clean transactions we have done before, these will be sloppy enough to trigger an investigation. One will conceal the skim for you. The rest... will point straight at Patrilla."

"You have always had a nose for trouble, eh?" Dubois said as he wiped his brow.

"And you always knew how to help," Manetti replied, sitting down.

Dubois gestured to the folder on the desk. "You want to ignite a fire with this, eh?"

"It's the fuse. But we have to configure it just right."

Dubois flipped through the binder again, moving more slowly now. His lips slightly parted as he read the amounts, the accounts, the routing slips. He paused on the Concordia page, recalling the day he'd built it with Manetti—a quiet afternoon in Miami Beach, a lunch that dragged on too long, and the smug satisfaction of outsmarting two compliance auditors in the same week.

Five million. The amount Manetti was offering. Enough to burn the bank's leash, pay for his future. Enough to be free.

But it wasn't just the money. Not really.

His exile still stung — not just because they had forced him out, but because it was over something he hadn't even done. A foolish yet costly financial mistake by a favored cousin he barely tolerated, brushed aside by the family at his expense. They'd whispered that "someone" had to take the fall. And the bank had agreed. Bimini was the polite term for banishment.

It had been an insult too deep to forgive. They'd stripped him of his standing, his pipeline to the boardroom, his seat at the family table. And here was Manetti, sliding the papers across the desk like a resurrection.

Dubois set the folder down and walked to the shutters, cracking them open wider. Outside, men aboard a fishing boat worked without hurry, patient, sure of their catch.

He turned back, weighing Manetti's offer in silence.

"They still use these, no?" Dubois asked.

"They use their bones. The structure still works."

"They trust you still?"

"They trust the system I built. They think I'm dead or have disappeared. I've become a ghost with administrative privileges."

Dubois leaned back. "So, what is the plan, eh?"

"We mimic one of our old laundering cycles. Create a phantom loop that looks real enough for a lazy clerk, but sloppy enough for a smart regulator to bite."

"And we make sure they bite?"

"Exactly," Manetti said as he showed Dubois the plan he had written. "Concordia sends \$3.7M to Trio Verde for 'feasibility studies.' Trio sends \$3.65M to Elmore for 'deployment analysis.' Then \$3.5M from Elmore to Petros Global in Miami 'settlement of prior obligations.'"

"And we shave the rest?"

"Five million to you, as agreed. Buried in a currency swap to your private account. Clean. Quiet. Yours.

"The balance to a Patrilla account in Manhattan. Closing the loop and pointing directly at them."

"This is not a small scheme, mon ami," Dubois said, his tone flatter now, but sharp around the edges. "This…is not one of our little shell games. If it fails, it will not be forgotten. Not by banks. Not by lawyers. Not by thugs."

"It won't fail," Manetti said.

Dubois gave a dry laugh. "I have heard that before."

"Not from me," Manetti said firmly.

"I work for a bank that hides cowards behind numbered accounts," he said finally. "Men like Abdullah. Like Patrilla. They trust men like me and you to clean their money and take the fall if needed. And what do I get, eh? Exile. Humiliation."

He lifted a brow.

"You know why I am here? Because of something I did.... nothing. The next month, poof, Bimini."

Manetti said nothing. He didn't have to. He was counting on such a response.

Dubois paced once, twice. Then stopped.

"You offer me five million, and a chance to spit in the eye of the men who made me disappear.

I have an old account in Tangier. Name of Jean-Luc Marchand. "I will resurrect it."

Dubois watched Manetti for a moment. Then nodded.

"If this goes wrong, it won't be only you, mon ami.."

Manetti stood and walked to the window. "It already went wrong. My old life is gone. Depending on how I handle this, my reputation will be ruined. People I care about are in the crosshairs. I can't run anymore. We'll build it to shield you, Emil. Later, if you need to, you and your family can disappear with your money."

Dubois picked up his pen, clicked it once.

A thin smile crept across his face.

"It's time we make the rules, no?"

He looked at Manetti, "We do it."

Dubois's voice hardened, "You realize, once it begins, there is no stopping it."

"I'm counting on that," Manetti said.

******

They spent the next few hours engineering the scheme.

Manetti loaded the aging, grey IBM Selectric with the transmittal memorandum documents provided by Dubois. Using his plan notes, account numbers, and passwords, he typed the specifics of each transaction and passed them to Emily to proofread.

Emily carefully reviewed each item, comparing Manettis' notes to the memos. She scanned for typos, transposition errors, names, and dates. Minor misspellings and missing or extra letters in names were not as critical, but transposing account numbers and mismatched banks would immediately trigger a rejection of the transaction, costing time and possibly raising suspicion before the wires were sent. Therefore, everything was double-checked.

Emily's attention to detail was evident. Among the memoranda she found and corrected were three transposition errors and four routing code separators, seven fatal errors averted. And two account name misspellings.

The trap was subtle. Invoices overlapped. Duplicate invoice numbers. Funds looped like a Möbius strip through three countries and back to a Patrilla holding account in Manhattan.

Like the postal system, once a letter entered the system, it was official and on its way. It only took one co-conspirator to verify a wire transfer authorization. Dubois bribed a compatriot for cooperation. Forged documents, compromised protocols, and system overrides made origins nearly impossible to trace.

If all went right, the money would move fast.

They skimmed $5 million and buried it in a currency swap through Dubai, wired to Dubois' Tangier account. Concealed, untraceable.

Emily's voice cut in, calm but strained. "Do we know how long transfers take? Time zones?"

"If we get the wires out late tonight, each time zone will have tomorrow morning to process before end-of-day," Manetti said. "If it hits a trigger too soon, during the transfer—SAR (Suspicious Activity Reports), AML(Anti-Money Laundering) audits, anything— that's flagged, the transfer will fail."

Dubois snorted. "Flagged? Non. We are burned, mon ami. Crisped. Barbecued."

With the stroke of the enter key at 11:23 p.m., the scheme was in motion. The first transfer was in the system.

Manetti stood over the terminal, arms crossed, jaw tight. Dubois paced, trailing wisps of harsh French cigarette smoke in his wake, suit jacket off, his white shirt clinging damp against his back. Emily sat on the edge of the desk, one foot tapping, eyes flickering between the two men.

"Now we wait," Manetti said.

CHAPTER 43

CANARY IN THE COAL MINE

Wednesday, December 19th

DUBOIS arrived at his usual time the next morning, with coffee and fresh croissants. He immediately walked through the now unoccupied office to his computer terminal, turned it on, and logged in.

Nothing yet. No rejections. No red flags. Yet no confirmations.

Manetti and Emily arrived at the bank at around 10:00 a.m. A young clerk greeted them at the door and led them to Dubois' office.

The trio waited by the computer for signals.

"It should have posted by now," Dubois muttered, glancing at the frozen screen. "Why so slow, eh? This part always takes too long."

"No glitches," Manetti said hopefully under his breath. "No errors."

They waited longer.

At 10:35 local time, a ping.

All three turned toward the screen.

The screen blinked once—then again.

Funds Transfer Confirmation #1

Originator Bank: Hamilton Trust Ltd. – Tortola, BVI

Beneficiary Bank: Curaçao Finance Bank – Willemstad, Curaçao

Date: December 19, 2001

Transaction ID: HTX390223578BV

Debiting Account: Concordia Real Estate Holdings Ltd. – ACCT# 1289-003291

Beneficiary Account: Trio Verde Capital – ACCT# 7410028762

Amount: $3,700,000.00 USD

Reference: Invoice #11297-B – Real Estate Feasibility Study – Project Echelon

Routing: SWIFT MT103 — with customer remittance information

Settlement Time: Same-day value

Currency: USD

FX Rate: N/A

Status: Settled

They exhaled. Not relief—just a breath. The real heat was still coming.

Dubois blew smoke toward the ceiling. "Wahn down. Trois to go."

Emily looked at Manetti. "If they spot the loop?"

"They won't, not yet," he said. "They're too busy looking for guns and drugs. Not ghosts in ledgers. We're counting on a compliance officer to catch it later."

Still, his fingers hovered just above the escape key, as if he could vanish it all with one press.

A second ping minutes later.

Funds Transfer Confirmation #2

Originator Bank: Curaçao Finance Bank – Willemstad, Curaçao
Beneficiary Bank: AlpenBank Liechtenstein – Vaduz, Liechtenstein
Date: December 19, 2001
Transaction ID: CFB9237751094
Debiting Account: Trio Verde Capital – ACCT# 7410028762
Beneficiary Account: Elmore Trading GmbH – ACCT# 55811-903-C
Amount: $3,650,000.00 USD
Reference: Strategic Deployment Analysis (SDA/Ref# 199-LA)
Routing: SWIFT MT103 + MT202
Settlement Time: Next-day value
Currency: USD
FX Rate: N/A
Status: Settled

"Now we wait for the one that matters to moi." Dubois said. "Tangier. If that one fails—"

"We're not thinking that way," Manetti cut him off.

Ten minutes later….

Funds Transfer Confirmation #3

Originator Bank: AlpenBank Liechtenstein – Vaduz, Liechtenstein
Beneficiary Bank: Banque Commerciale du Maghreb – Tangier, Morocco
Date: December 19, 2001
Transaction ID: ABLI-TGN00201547
Debiting Account: Elmore Trading GmbH – ACCT# 55811-903-C
Beneficiary Account: Jean-Luc Marchand – ACCT# 44021-

89913-17

Amount: $5,000,000.00 USD

Reference: Currency Conversion Settlement – SWAP-1094A/ Dirham

Routing: SWIFT MT103 — Currency code MAD

Conversion: USD to MAD @ 1 USD = 11.62 MAD

Settlement Time: T+2

Currency Delivered: Moroccan Dirham

FX Net: 58,100,000.00 MAD

Status: Confirmed – Confidential Client Tag Applied

Manetti cracked his knuckles. Emily crossed herself, then smirked at her reflex.

Dubois stubbed out his cigarette and lit another.

"Tres bien!" Dubois exclaimed with a broad smile.

Minutes passed.

Then the cursor blinked twice.

International Wire Transfer Confirmation

Transaction ID: PGNY-TRF09210165

Date of Execution: December 18, 2001

Settlement Date: December 19, 2001 (T+0)

ORIGINATOR BANK:

Petros Global Private Bank

Suite 1802, Brickell Financial Center

Miami, FL 33131

SWIFT/BIC: PETGUS33

SENDING PARTY (Remitter):

Elmore Trading GmbH

Industriestrasse 8, Vaduz, Liechtenstein

Account #: 55811-903-C

Bank Reference #: 4210/ET-VADUZ

BENEFICIARY BANK:

Manhattan Bridge Bank

Corporate Services Division

485 Lexington Avenue

New York, NY 10017

SWIFT/BIC: MBBKUS44

BENEFICIARY PARTY:

Mid-town Realty Holdings, Inc.

Account #: 0214-905717

Bank Reference #: MTRH-NY-MBB-01

Client ID: 07-091-MR-2001

AMOUNT TRANSFERRED:

USD $3,500,000.00

Currency: United States Dollars

Transfer Type: MT103 SWIFT Wire

Value Date: Same-day

Status: Settled

The room went still for a beat. No sound but the fan above.

Then, softly, Emily: "We did it."

Dubois grinned, yellow teeth beneath the smoke. "Bienvenue, welcome to Hell, mes amis."

Manetti finally let himself breathe. "Let's hope they bite."

Dubois moved to the computer on his desk and logged into his Tangier account.

A $5 million deposit had cleared overnight.

"Relief, mon amis, the transfer is complete to my account," exclaims Dubois.

Immediately and surreptitiously, he transferred the entire amount to a blind Brazilian account kept secret from Manetti, further hiding the transaction from claw-back.

Dubois, with an exit plan and the fuse lit, poured three glasses of Kentucky bourbon, raised his glass, and toasted the only man who could make him nervous.

"To old ghosts, mon amis" he said.

"To canaries in coal mines," Manetti replied.

******

Two days later, at Petros Global Bank, Miami, a recent international transaction caught the eye of a compliance officer; a ledger entry with duplicate invoice numbers flagged for observation.

Lara Kim, Petros Global, Brickell branch. A fresh bank hire from the Financial Crimes Enforcement Network (FinCEN) with good instincts.

She spotted an anomaly in supporting documents - invoice #11297-B. Same number, different dates. Different companies.

She flagged the account for more scrutiny. Filed a SAR with Treasury. Then a memo to the Feds. Red flags went up.

Attached to the original wire:

PAYMENT DETAILS:

Settlement of Prior Obligations — Contract Ref: MTRH/09/01A

Wire authorized by: C. Hasler (Compliance Officer)

Compliance Notes: KYC Complete | Low-Risk Jurisdiction |

Transaction flagged for internal review by AML Review Desk (File Ref: 918/PG-BB) due to repeated invoice code.

Compliance Stamp:
☐ Flagged by Petros Global AML Unit – File Retained under SAR Audit Queue
☐ Retention Category: 180-Day Observation

Within a week, men in dark suits sat in the Petros Global branch manager's office, requesting transaction histories and names.

The account belonged to a holding company in Liechtenstein. The funds benefit a Manhattan real estate company, Midtown Realty Holdings, which is controlled by Anthony Patrilla.

The trail hit smoke there.

Compliance office Lara Kim commented, "Somebody got stupid, or very sloppy."

The fuse was lit.

CHAPTER 44

THE "CONTRIBUTION"

Thursday, December 20th

THE morning after lighting the fuse on the Patrilla family, the trio gathered in Dubois' office. The island air was sharp with salt and the hush of consequence. Outside, gulls cut across a blue sky like warning signs. The celebration from the night before was over. Manetti had one more target in mind.

"Next," Manetti said, as he dropped a thick folder onto Dubois' desk, "we shine a light on the man who bankrolled the 9/11 attack: Sheikh Ziad Abdullah."

Dubois raised a brow, but said nothing.

"These two accounts"—Manetti tapped the folder— "hold north of three-quarters of a billion dollars. Only two people outside the sheikh's inner circle knew about the account or had authority over it: me and Willoughby. He's MIA. I'm supposed to be dead."

He paused to let the implication settle.

"We're going to drain them…fast. The funds get routed to the 9/11 Victims' Fund. The math comes out to $250,000 for each victim. By sundown, the money lands. Courtesy of the sheikh."

Emily looked toward Dubois for a reaction. Saw his jaw ease, but he said nothing

"No money repays what was taken," Manetti continued. "But this—this humiliates them. And it's only the beginning."

He slid a piece of paper across the desk.

"Press release. Already prepped for delivery to the *New York Tribune*. When I give the signal, it's on the editor's desk. By the time he reads and confirms it, the wire transfer's a done deal."

Emily leaned forward to glance at the press release as Dubois picked it up and silently scanned the contents.

The House of Abdullah expresses its profound sorrow for the tragic events of September 11, 2001. In the spirit of brotherhood, we offer this contribution of $744,000,000 to the United States 9/11 Victims' Fund in honor of the innocent lives lost, and as a gesture of enduring solidarity between our peoples.

—Sheikh Ziad Abdullah, Riyadh, Kingdom of Saudi Arabia

Dubois snorted.

"This is outrageous; it's not a confession. It's a ruse."

"Yes, it's a trap," Manetti said. "And a memorial."

Emily frowned. "Who delivers the letter?"

"Anonymous," Manetti replied.

He tapped another folder.

"That one's Naseem Holdings. Abdullah's primary laundering front. It paid for fake passports, flight schools, and phone cards. It paid for bringing down the towers."

Dubois stared at the folder, eyes flat. Then turned away.

"You told me this was not political."

"It's not," Manetti said. "It's personal."

"I was there. I was also used, as you already know. It's even possible my firm was chosen as an intermediary because our offices were in those buildings. A convenient target to wipe out any evidence of Simon & Kershaw's involvement with the sheikh. I've given that some thought, but have no proof."

Emily stepped forward. "What now?"

"Essentially, we're ready to go," Manetti said. "I just need Emil's cooperation."

Dubois stood at the window, backlit by the Caribbean sun glare filtering through the open shutters. He clutched the folder labeled Naseem Holdings tightly, as though it carried weight beyond paper.

Emily remained seated, composed, watching him carefully. Manetti leaned forward.

Dubois turned slowly, the file still in his hand.

Manetti continued. "Emil… you know the work we've done. What I've done. I didn't care where the money came from—dirty or clean. I got paid. That was enough.

"But after the attacks…," Manetti continued… "after what happened…. this stopped being just numbers on a wire. These bastards murdered thousands. I helped hide their money. Whether I knew it or not—I helped."

Dubois turned, slowly.

"That is what you feel, mon ami. But the risk? Your feelings do not belong to me. I am not American. If they come knocking, I do not have the luxury of waving a flag and demanding a lawyer."

"I get it," Manetti said. "But you're not a target. You're a name on a form. All you're doing is processing instructions from an authorized signature. You don't benefit directly. The account gets drained, and the press does the rest."

"But it's your war, not mine," Dubois said. "I did not lose friends in the towers. I was not there when the ash fell. What do I gain? What makes this my fight?"

Manetti paused. Emily spoke instead.

"You said you have children, Emil."

"Oui. A daughter."

Emily leaned forward. "Then maybe this isn't about our war. Maybe it's about the next one. Men like Abdullah don't stop with one atrocity—they bankroll the next, and the next, until someone takes away their purse. Every transfer you run for him, every dollar that sits untouched in that account, funds the next blade, the next bomb, the next fatherless child. Maybe you don't carry our flag, but you do carry your name. And if you do nothing, Emil, one day you may have to tell your daughter you stood aside when you could have acted."

Her words hung in the stillness. Dubois' jaw worked as though chewing on something bitter. He looked at the folder again, thumb tracing the edge.

He turned back to the window, almost speaking to himself. "In my country, long ago, the occupiers wore gray coats and polite smiles. They paid well, and some took their money, saying, 'It is not our war.' And when it ended, the ones who stood aside were remembered no better than the ones who collaborated."

He exhaled slowly, his shoulders settling as if the decision carried both weight and release. "Perhaps this is not my war, Emily. But maybe it is my chance to choose the right side before history is written."

Dubois faced them fully now. "I will need the documentation. Every signature. Every date. You will blind me, yes?"

"Absolutely," Manetti said. "You'll be cleaner than a Swiss vault. We set up the fall. When the time's right, we pull the thread and let it all come loose."

Dubois poured three glasses of water from a sweating pitcher. "You have proof, mon ami, no?"

"You have my word. My story. My guilt. And Willoughby's forged signature authorizing the wire. I'll transmit it from the mainland. It'll leave Emil clean.", as he turned toward Emily.

"And the Saudis?" Dubois asked.

"This won't bring Abdullah down alone—but it will stain him. Publicly and privately. The Royal Court will take notice too. And the money—seven hundred million—it's noise to him. That's a weekend's revenue from oil."

But the press release will force his hand. He'll own it. The Saudis are already under suspicion."

Dubois looked at Emily. Then back to Manetti.

"And if it goes wrong?"

Manetti said. "You walk with clean hands. A hero, even."

"The bastards hide behind numbered accounts. And they *still* sleep in palaces." Dubois said as an aside.

"So it is vengeance, not justice," Dubois continued.

"It's remembrance," Manetti said.

Emily's voice was soft and resolute as she turned to Manetti, "And whatever comes, we move forward, together."

Dubois considered it. His face gave nothing away. He gave a small nod. Then he raised his glass.

"To the satisfaction of revenge. Let us see how far your madness can reach."

Manetti touched his glass to Emil's and said, "To remembering what they'd rather we forget."

CHAPTER 45

TRIGGER EFFECT

Friday, December 21st

THE morning sunlight danced off the glass and steel that framed Lower Manhattan. Inside the U.S. Attorney's Office for the Southern District of New York, Ava Ramirez sipped lukewarm coffee from a reusable travel mug, scanning a fresh batch of compliance alerts forwarded from FinCEN's Transaction Monitoring Unit in Manhattan.

One in particular made her freeze.

She leaned in closer, examining the string again. The flagged transaction originated from an offshore account associated with a Tortola, BVI-based shipping subsidiary known to be tied to Patrilla Holdings—a front entity already on her radar. But this transfer wasn't routine. The amount—$3.7 million USD — was not large, but the structuring, timing, and routing through a Curacao bank via two-layered accounts to a U.S. bank all pointed to one thing: suspicious.

She clicked open the transaction trail—internal references, coded identifiers, and the exchange protocol embedded in the

Society for Worldwide Interbank Financial Telecommunications (SWIFT) message. Someone had spread breadcrumbs.

"Holy hell," Ava muttered.

She opened her encrypted email with Gallagher's administrative assistant.

A.R.: "Need to see Gallagher. Five minutes. Tell her it's about Manetti."

S.Z.: "On it. Gallagher's free in 15."

Ava snatched the printouts and strode down the hallway toward Justine Gallagher's corner office. She knocked once.

Gallagher looked up from her laptop. "Come in, Ava."

"Something just came in flagged by FinCEN's New York office," Ava said, spreading the documents across Gallagher's glass-top desk. "Wire transfers routed through Tortola, originating from a shell under Patrilla Holdings. This one's screaming for attention. Routing anomalies, bad layering, and the destination account was opened in 1997, but has had little activity in the last year or so."

Gallagher leaned in, reading the pathing. "This was intentional, not sloppy," she said.

Ava nodded. "It's bait. And I think Manetti is behind it."

Gallagher sat back. "Jesus, he moved fast."

"He's serious. He wants us to bite," Ava said. "I cross-referenced it against raw data from the Simon & Kershaw preliminary inquiry— unusual transactions, offshore banks, even internal routing nomenclature. It matches the pattern."

Gallagher tapped her fingers on the table, her mind racing.

"You think this is enough to open?"

Ava's voice was calm but firm. "If we don't, we're missing what may be our only shot."

Gallagher exhaled sharply. "Alright. Call Park in here."

Nathan Park arrived minutes later, tie slightly loosened, holding a legal pad.

"We have movement," Gallagher told him. "Rossi's informant—he's serious. Ava's found a transaction staged as bait. Patrilla funds; offshore transfer. Designed to fire us up."

Nathan scanned the pages Ava handed him. "Well, that's... bold."

Gallagher nodded. "It's what we asked for."

"What's the timeline on the transaction?"

"Less than 72 hours ago," Ava replied. "He's not wasting time."

Gallagher turned to Park. "Open a case file. Flag it Level Three."

Nathan scribbled the header.

Gallagher stood. "I want to meet this guy asap."

Park hesitated. "We still don't have confirmation of exactly who he is."

"Rossi does," Gallagher said. "He's our bridge. Reach out. Let him know we'll entertain an immunity offer contingent on a formal proffer and material review."

Ava interjected. "He gave us a pattern. If he can explain the architecture used in their other transactions, provide more documentation, and testimony, then we might have our scaffolding for money laundering and RICO charges."

Nathan raised an eyebrow. "Tied directly to Sonny?"

"Especially Sonny," Gallagher said.

Ava flipped through her notes. "There are other accounts linked to this same pipeline. If he has access, we can verify control. I'd want to see originating docs—beneficial ownership trails, correspondence, authorizations."

Gallagher turned back to Park. "Make sure Rossi knows this won't be a fishing expedition. We'll need names, dates, accounts, actions. Anything less than that, the offer's DOA."

"I'll draft the proffer and get it to Rossi." Park offered.

Ava collected the files. "Should I alert FinCEN we're taking jurisdiction?"

"Yes. Quietly. And loop in our cyber team. If the informant accessed the accounts remotely, I want full packet traces."

Park glanced up. "What about the question of credibility?"

Gallagher didn't blink. "If he pulled this off without setting off Patrilla's people, he's already credible."

She looked to Ava. "Set a timeline. I want a meeting within a week. We don't sit on this."

Ava nodded. "Understood."

******

Late that evening, in his Trenton apartment, Rocco Rossi read the email from Gallagher, jaw tightening with mixed relief and anticipation.

We saw the wire. If it's him, tell him it worked. Park will be in touch with terms. Meeting within the week. No promises yet. But he has our attention. Justine

Rossi leaned back into the worn leather chair in his small living room. He'd been wondering how much longer Manetti would stay one step ahead of the storm.

He typed a message and sent it to Andrea's email.

Andrea, tell your brother: The U.S. Attorney's office wants to meet. If Michael engineered a wire—it was brilliant and got their attention.

I don't know the details, but Gallagher's on board for a meeting. Likely within a week. Will follow up. Tell him to be ready. And cautious. Rossi

******

In a sunlit booth at the back of a Key West diner later that afternoon, Manetti read Rossi's earlier message regarding Gallagher's reply. Emily sat beside him, her fingers resting over his hand. They had just returned from Bimini.

"Did it work?" she asked, voice low.

He nodded. "It worked. Brilliantly, according to Rossi. They want to meet.

When the Abdullah news hits, the timetable will move up fast."

Emily let out a breath, unsure if she should be relieved or afraid.

"You're really going through with this," she said.

Manetti looked her in the eyes. "I have to."

He thought about the faces—Zaid Abdullah's manipulations, Sonny Patrilla's clipped voice on calls from burner phones. Every document, every ledger, every offshore account—they were pieces of a truth long buried.

Now he was digging them up.

CHAPTER 46

THE DROP

Friday afternoon, December 21st

WHILE cruising back to Key West on Friday morning, the *Kitty Jo* stopped in Key Largo to refuel. Manetti walked several blocks inland to a public library. Amidst flickering fluorescent lights and aging Dell desktops, he took a terminal near the stacks and opened his folder.

The transfer instructions and protocols were documented; Willoughby's forged signature was attached to the authorization letter, and instructions to Société Française Suisse Banque were checked and double-checked. Manetti hesitated… only a moment. Then pressed SEND.

Dubois knew what to do when the transaction order hit his desk.

The next message Manetti sent was to the Lazarus dead drop email address.

"Andi, copy the following letter. Use plain white paper. Delete this message when finished. Use a plain envelope, no stamp, no return address. No identification whatsoever. Disguise yourself. Hand-deliver asap today

or tomorrow to the lobby desk at the NY Tribune. Acknowledge when done through this drop. Then watch the news unfold." Love M.

******

The air on the Manhattan street smelled of wet concrete and roasted chestnuts. Sidewalks glistened from recent rain. Steam hissed up from the subway grates. Everything moved quickly, with purpose.

Andrea Manetti stepped off the 7th Ave. subway platform at Times Square, swallowed by the lunchtime crowd. A wide-brimmed hat rested low, obscuring her features. Just another face in the blur of Midtown foot traffic.

As she walked east toward the *New York Tribune* building, her boots echoed faintly on the pavement. The city buzzed around her—vendors shouting over food carts; delivery trucks double-parked with engines idling; taxi horns honking in quick bursts. The smell of street pretzels mingled with exhaust fumes. It was familiar. It was impersonal. It was Manhattan.

The Tribune stood like a granite sentinel at the corner of Sixth and West 44th—broad and dignified, its limestone columns darkened with age. The revolving doors were polished, the brass handles dulled by years of anxious palms. A security guard could be seen inside, sipping coffee behind a marble lobby desk. Overhead, a brass chandelier flickered with tired bulbs.

Andrea paused across the street. Heart pounding. She reached into her bag and touched the envelope again; its weight was far heavier with her anxiety.

Handwritten in block letters:

Editor – New York Tribune – URGENT

No return address. No stamp. No trace.

Earlier at Beans & Bytes, Andrea checked the inbox of the Lazarus email address, waiting for any news from her brother. Disappointed that there was no personal update and stunned by the message she received, she read it twice. She then printed the letter as instructed and bought a plain white envelope at the counter.

Now she exhaled, crossed the street, and stepped through the revolving door.

Inside, a security camera blinked overhead. A custodian buffed the marble floor. A woman in a red blazer flipped through a clipboard. Phones rang in short, bureaucratic bursts.

Andrea approached the reception desk. Her voice was low, steady.

"For the editor," she said. "It's urgent."

The man behind the counter didn't look up. Just motioned toward the message slot in the marble counter. She slipped the envelope through the slot.

"Thank you," she said.

The man nodded once. Already answering a phone. She was forgotten before the glass door whispered shut behind her.

Back on the street, Andrea headed west toward Times Square. At the corner of 45th, she slipped into a small internet café. Rows of old terminals flickered in a dim room that smelled of smoke and overheated plastic.

She slipped quarters into the coin box and logged in. The Lazarus account blinked alive.

Her fingers hovered over the keyboard, then typed: *"Mission accomplished."*

She logged out and walked into the blur of early afternoon

******

On Bimini, in a back office of Société Française Suisse Banque that afternoon, a wire officer supervised by Dubois logged the requests into the system. She verified each document, checked the header codes, and confirmed the formatting and authentication protocols. Everything seemed in order. Dubois signed the acceptance himself.

Per the instructions, the transfers would execute before the end of the business day, Friday, December 21st.

******

By the time Andrea's boots emerged from the taxi and touched the wet pavement again near her apartment, the trap was already set.

Manetti read her reply, smiled, chuckled, then deleted it.

Within 24 hours, two Saudi-controlled accounts would be $744 million lighter.

And the world was about to learn of Sheikh Ziad Abdullah's "contribution."

Before calling it a night, Rossi opened the Lazarus account—just to check.

One message.

This time, the previous draft hadn't been deleted.

Andrea had replied quickly with "Mission accomplished" written plainly. But above it, still sitting open, was Manetti's latest message. Rossi clicked the cursor and began to read.

It was the text of a bomb shell letter—one purportedly designed to have come from Sheikh Zaid Abdullah himself.

Rossi blinked, then read it again.

"This guy must be out of his mind," Rossi muttered, leaning back.

"What does Manetti have on this guy?"

He hovered over the "Print" button, then stopped. Not yet. Not until he knew where this was going.

The letter and the funds transfer, if genuine—and if they even reached the *New York Tribune*—would ignite a firestorm. Legally, politically, internationally. The kind of firestorm that would put Manetti directly in the crosshairs of people more dangerous than Patrilla.

Rossi closed the laptop, heart drumming, knowing something big could happen in a few days. Best to sit on it. For now.

CHAPTER 47

THE TRIBUNE NEWSROOM

Afternoon, Friday, December 21st

O N the sixth floor of the *New York Tribune*'s aging headquarters—an eight-story limestone block on West 44th Street—the early evening light cast no shadows through the grimy casement windows, illuminating cluttered desks with old Rolodexes, corkboards, and half-eaten sandwiches wrapped in wax paper. As the Christmas holiday weekend approached, the newsroom buzzed with the clatter of keyboards, the soft murmur of landline phones, and the distant hum of delivery trucks crawling down Sixth Avenue. Cigarette smoke still faintly lingered on the walls, a ghost of decades past.

Trib senior investigative reporter, Martin Karsh, leaned back in a creaky office chair, nursing a black coffee, watching the newsroom through horn-rimmed glasses. His desk was a cluttered battlefield of manila folders, Post-it notes, and a dented Olympus microcassette recorder. The overhead fluorescents buzzed faintly.

Near the elevators, the mail boy—seventeen, pimply, and listening to Nine Inch Nails on a Walkman—pushed his wheeled cart along the corridor of editors' offices and reporters' desks, tossing envelopes onto desks with barely a glance. At the door marked "Elliot Samuelson – Managing Editor," he paused, delivered the late afternoon mail and internal memos, and then disappeared down the hall.

Samuelson, silver-haired and heavyset, an icon from the Watergate era, newspaperman, sat hunched over, sleeves rolled up, his red suspenders stretched tight. He thumbed through the stack absentmindedly—readers complaining about bias, a shiny promo from a PR firm, a packet from the crossword editor.

Then he saw it: white envelope, plain, drugstore quality. All-caps: "URGENT." No return address. No stamp.

He slit it with a brass letter opener.

Read it once. Then again. His brows lowered.

"What the hell is this?"

He picked up the phone. "Sara," he barked. "Come in here."

A moment later, Sara Hollister entered, notebook in hand, blonde hair pulled back tight. She was young, efficient, and sharp.

"Take this to Karsh," he said, handing her the letter. "Tell him to check it out. First, call the 9/11 Victims' Fund and ask if they've received anything unusual. If yes, he gets on the phone with the Saudis—see if their consulate has a comment. And if there's a story here, I want it in the Sunday edition. Center spread. No delays."

Sara nodded and disappeared down the hall.

Martin Karsh read the letter with the jaded detachment of a man who had seen everything from embezzlement scandals to illegal CIA experiments. Still, something about the simplicity of the message, the magnitude—$744 million—made his pulse tick faster.

"Anonymous," he muttered. "Of course."

He looked at the clock. 5:17 p.m. The start of the Christmas holiday. Dinner reservations at Le Colonial with his wife. Already pushing it.

He picked up the phone. Called Judy Schmidt, executive assistant to the director of the 9/11 Victims' Fund.

"Hey Jude," he said when she answered on the third ring.

"Martin. You caught me on my way out the door. What's up?"

"We got a weird one. Anonymous drop at the Trib. Letter claims the 9/11 Victims' Fund just got a wire—big one."

"How big?"

"Seven hundred forty-four million."

Silence. Then a soft whistle.

"You're kidding."

"I wish. That's Saudi oil money, Jude. The name on the letter is Sheikh Ziad Abdullah. You ever hear of him?"

"No, but I've had smaller checks from private donors in the Gulf region. I'd have remembered that one."

"If it turns up, I want the call first. Can you do that for me?"

"You'll be the first. Hell, the world will know—but I'll give you a head start."

"Appreciate it. Enjoy your weekend."

Karsh hung up and looked again at the letter. If it was true—if it was real—it was the biggest human-interest money story since the attacks. It had teeth. It had mystery. It had blood.

Monday, December 24th – Christmas Eve Morning

Judy Schmidt had just set her coffee down when her desk line rang. She picked up.

"Schmidt," she answered.

"Judy, it's Hank at Columbia Trust. You're gonna want to sit down."

"I'm already sitting, Hank. What is it?"

"A wire came through over the weekend. Cleared this morning. The amount's real."

"How much?"

"Seven hundred forty-four million. Even."

Silence. Then: "Sender?"

"Two separate accounts. Société Française Suisse Banque. The sender IDs match a known Saudi holding company—Naseem Holdings. Offshore, but the source looks clean. We verified against the clearinghouse protocols."

"Confirmation papers?"

"Already faxed to your office. Merry Christmas!"

Judy hung up and stared at the receiver for a second. Then she picked up the phone again and punched Karsh's number.

In the Tribune Newsroom

Karsh answered on the first ring. "Talk to me."

"Marty," Judy said, her voice half disbelief, half adrenaline. "It's real."

He sat forward.

"What?"

"The wire. It hit. Two accounts. $744 million. From a Saudi company. Naseem Holdings."

Karsh exhaled slowly. "Holy shit."

"You have your story," Schmidt says.

"And the world has a headline," Karsh replied.

He was already reaching for his Rolodex, for reliable sources and comments.

CHAPTER 48

THE NEW YORK TRIBUNE

Monday, December 24th Christmas Eve

THE headline of The *New York Tribune* Evening Edition read:
Saudi Sheikh Donates $744 Million to 9/11 Victim Fund
Private Gift Called "Gesture of Brotherhood" from Sheikh Zaid
Abdullah

By Martin Karsh | Exclusive

In a historic act of solidarity and humanitarian effort, Sheikh
Zaid Abdullah, a well-known Saudi businessman and philanthropist,
made a personal donation of $744 million to the 9/11 Victims' Fund.
The Tribune confirmed that the contribution has been received.

The donation, transferred in full by wire to the designated
victim's fund charitable bank account early Monday, was announced
in a letter left with the editor of the *New York Tribune*, not yet
authenticated, from Sheikh Abdullah, expressing "deep sorrow"
for the lives lost in New York, Washington, and Pennsylvania during
the recent terror attacks. The text of the letter follows:

"The people of Saudi Arabia share in the grief of our American

brothers and sisters," the letter reads. "As a father, a Muslim, and a human being, I mourn the innocent lives extinguished by this barbarity. This gesture is not enough—but it is sincere."

According to FBI sources, the amount comes to about $250,000 per acknowledged victim, based on an estimate of 2977 deaths from the four attacks. Although the donation was made privately and not on behalf of the Kingdom of Saudi Arabia, it has already sparked worldwide discussion.

White House Press Secretary Casey Harrington issued a brief statement in response, saying, "The generosity of Sheikh Abdullah, like the generosity of so many around the world, reflects the shared values of decency, compassion, and resolve."

When asked for further comment, the press secretary declined to elaborate.

Zaid Abdullah, 58, is known internationally for his energy and mineral investments and philanthropic ventures. His foundation, the Z.A. Trust, has previously supported education and clean water projects across Africa and the Gulf region.

This marks the largest individual foreign donation ever received by a U.S. disaster relief initiative.

An Abdullah family spokesperson said that an official press conference would be forthcoming. No official press conference has been scheduled.

******

Trenton was dressed for Christmas. Strands of white lights sagged as they hung between weathered telephone poles, and wreaths decorated every city lamppost along Broad Street. A steady stream of last-minute shoppers hurried between storefronts, heads tucked against the cold. Rocco Rossi moved like a man on a mission—his breath puffing in short bursts in the December air as he scanned the shelves inside Quinn's Books and News.

He wasn't there for bestsellers.

In one hand, he held a gift bag from Lacey's Toy Store across the street; inside was a new fire truck for his grandson, Luca, who, pleasing Rossi, had recently declared he wanted to be a firefighter "just like the ones that saved New York." In the other hand, he held a brown paper envelope containing a gift certificate for his daughter's favorite Italian bakery. Nothing fancy, just enough to show he was thinking of them.

As he reached for a pack of cigarettes near the register, a headline caught his eye from the corner display stand: The *New York Tribune*, hot off the press. A bold, impossible-to-miss headline above the fold, stretching across the front page:

Saudi Sheikh Donates $744 Million to 9/11 Victim Fund

Rossi froze. Time stopped for a beat, his body rigid under the weight of disbelief.

He grabbed the paper and flipped it open, scanning with laser focus.

Rossi read the article and the text of the letter. The letter was identical to the one he had read in the Lazarus inbox three days earlier.

His jaw dropped. A small paper cup of steaming coffee in his hand tilted just enough to spill, and Rossi, distracted, barely reacted as the hot liquid hit his glove and splashed onto the counter.

"Shit," he muttered, grabbing napkins, his hands shaking slightly.

The clerk gave him a sideways glance, but Rossi was already

digging for his wallet.

"Coffee, the paper," he said hoarsely. "And the cigarettes."

He stepped onto the sidewalk, clutching *The Tribune* tightly under one arm. The wind gusted harder now. His thoughts swirled like a snow squall inside his head.

He walked briskly back to his parked car, tossed the shopping bags onto the passenger seat, and sat behind the wheel. He turned the ignition key and headed home.

The letter had made it. The funds had moved. It was real.

He let out a long, low whistle. "You crazy son of a bitch," he whispered. "You actually did it."

The audacity of the move stunned him. Manetti wasn't just leaving breadcrumbs anymore. He was pouring gasoline onto the floor and lighting a match.

Back at his apartment, Rossi dropped the bags by the door and booted his computer. The apartment had a faint evergreen scent, the latent aroma from the "holiday" spray on the artificial tree in the corner. He didn't even bother removing his coat.

He opened the Lazarus account. No new messages. Closed the file and opened his email account.

He cursed under his breath and began composing a message to Andrea's private email.

Andrea, did Michael have anything to do with the Abdullah wire story? If so, I need to talk to him. Tell him to call me ASAP.

—Rossi

He hit send and stared at the screen. The silence in the apartment grew heavier, as if waiting with him for an answer that could upend everything.

Rossi leaned back in his chair, arms crossed, eyes scanning the headlines again.

The article was already blowing up on cable news. Speculation ran rampant. Treasury was "reviewing the transaction." A spokesperson from the White House had "no additional comments." Some outlets were calling it an act of contrition. Others, a hoax. No one could confirm the origin.

But Rossi knew. He'd seen the draft. He had read the words.

Now the world had too.

And if Gallagher thought the Bimini wire transfer was enough to get her attention, this... this would set her whole building on fire.

He muttered to himself, "You'd better know what you're doing, Michael."

Because if not, there wouldn't be a safe harbor left—FBI, SDNY, witness protection, or otherwise.

The storm Manetti had been dancing around had just gone from offshore squall to full hurricane. And it was headed right for him.

CHAPTER 49

EMPIRE UNDONE

Christmas morning, December 25, 2001

The *New York Tribune* headline:

SAUDI DONATION STUNS THE WORLD

Fund Windfall Triggers Scrutiny — Is There More To The Story?

By Martin Karsh | Tribune Investigations

Above the fold, Karsh laid out the transfer details, quotes from stunned sources at the 9/11 Fund, a canned statement from the Saudi embassy—"We are reviewing this matter"—and a sharp paragraph quoting Treasury Department officials who had "no prior knowledge" of the contribution and were "opening an internal review to assess source compliance."

The article set off the expected firestorm.

Cable news ran with it by noon. CNN led with "Mystery Billionaire's Gift," while Fox News demanded a conspiracy investigation. MSNBC panels speculated on motive, terrorism financing, and whether the Saudis were trying to buy goodwill—or cover something up.

At the White House, a statement of "neither confirming nor

denying" became the top item at the afternoon press briefing. The Press Secretary awkwardly dodged questions about what this meant for U.S.-Saudi relations.

In a Key West motel room, Manetti read the news with unease. *Have I done the right thing?* he asked himself.

******

Riyadh, Saudi Arabia

The private villa in the Diplomatic Quarter was ringed by tamarisk trees and guarded by Royal Protection officers. Inside, cool marble floors muted the *madas sharqi* footsteps of a small circle of men who gathered beneath ornate archways and an elaborate chandelier.

The majlis was quiet—except for the rustle of a newspaper. A single copy of the *Washington Courier*'s front page lay open on a low table.

$744 MILLION DONATION TO 9/11 VICTIM FUND

Sheikh Ziad Abdullah, seated in a tailored grey thobe, stared at the page like it was a warrant for his arrest.

Two of his most trusted aides stood nearby—Jamil Abadi, head of legal affairs, and Karim Omar, a former intelligence officer turned political fixer. A third man, Nasir Saleh, a financial strategist to multiple Gulf royals, sat across from him with a laptop on his knees.

Jamil Abadi broke the silence.

" Your Excellency... this story has already reached CNN, Al Jazeera, and the *Financial Times*. Every outlet is now repeating it. And we've confirmed the wire went through. Full amount.

Karim Omar added in a low voice, "The American fund has

acknowledged the deposit. Treasury has not publicly commented. But there are inquiries. It's only a matter of time before they investigate how the funds moved."

Ziad exhaled through his nose. Cold and controlled.

"I never authorized this."

"No, Excellency," Nasir Saleh said. "But someone did. The wire originated from Naseem Holdings."

Ziad's jaw clenched.

"Naseem is buried. How did it leak?"

"Unknown," said Saleh. "Possibly an insider. Possibly a breach."

"Or an enemy," Omar muttered

"The New York law firm we used for some of our offshore accounts, including Naseem Holdings, was Simon & Kershaw. We chose them because of the vulnerability of one of the partners, Christopher Willoughby," Saleh stated as he referred to his notes. "Willoughby was deemed malleable and susceptible to influence. Also, the firm was in one of the Twin Towers. We knew all files and connections to you would be destroyed in the attack—an insurance against exposure.

"Suspiciously, the transaction documents were signed by Willoughby. For one thing, he is supposed to be dead, along with most of the staff and attorneys. Secondly, if he is alive and did do it, why? He had nothing to gain. The truth of his complicity would eventually be exposed."

Ziad stood slowly and walked to the window, one hand behind his back.

"I want the damage contained. Immediately."

Abadi spoke next. "There are two fronts, Excellency.

International—and domestic."

"Go on."

"Internationally, denying the transfer would be... unwise. The Americans will demand to know who sent it and why. Their media will not let this go. And if Treasury initiates a formal inquiry..."

"They will," Omar interrupted.

Abadi continued, "—then Naseem Holdings and any affiliated accounts could be exposed, possibly others."

Ziad turned from the window. "So, I cannot deny it."

"No," said Nasir. "But you can own it."

A beat of silence.

Saleh nodded slowly. "The press release. That language spoke of *grief, mourning,* and *brotherhood;* it is ready-made. Admit to the donation. Claim it as a private gesture of healing. You'll be called a humanitarian. Generous and compassionate. No one will question the motive—at least not publicly."

Ziad studied them all. "And the royal court?"

Saleh hesitated. "They... are watching. They do not want scrutiny either. But you must meet with the Committee of Finance and Allegiance privately. Explain it was a personal gesture. Say you were advised by your philanthropic board."

"And if they question the other accounts?"

"Freeze them yourself," Karim said quickly. "Initiate a quiet audit. Cooperate. Act preemptively. If you appear cooperative, the committee may preserve your status."

Ziad sat again. "And the Americans?"

Abadi spoke with care. "This gift will make you look benevolent. It may blunt the knives—briefly. But there will be a trail. Someone wants this to lead somewhere. It won't end here."

Ziad's eyes narrowed. "Then find out who."

Omar, the sheikh's intelligence chief, leaned in. "Willoughby had an associate, Michael Manetti, who handled much of the work. Both have been flagged previously by the Department of Justice in an ongoing wire transfer probe. Apparently, they handled accounts for Cosa Nostra families, of which we were not previously aware. The probe is tied to one of those families.

"To cover our tracks, as the Americans would say, I sent an operative three weeks ago to determine the legitimacy of their deaths in the attack. To find any evidence that one or both could be alive. Anything that could lead us to them.

"Willoughby had a family. Evidence points to his death. There was a funeral. No unusual activity. No travel. Surveillance of his home and tracking his widow's and children's movements has been fruitless. It appears she is in mourning and acting accordingly.

"Manetti had no family except for a sister. No funeral. Nothing.

"Those are the last reports. My operative's handler says contact from him is overdue. We are becoming suspicious."

Ziad said the names once, quietly. Then again.

"Keep looking. And if they're not dead… silence them."

He looked at Omar.

"Draft the press statement. We will hold a briefing at the embassy in London. I want sympathetic coverage. *Wall Street Journal. The Times of London. Al-Arabiya.*"

He turned toward the paper again, a flicker of distaste behind the eyes.

"I did not build an empire to be humbled by ghosts."

CHAPTER 50

SMOKE SIGNALS

THE fax machine in the back office of Sonny Patrilla's private suite at the Mirador Hotel & Casino in Atlantic City coughed out the final page.

Sonny stood still. White cuffs rolled to his elbows. Cigar smoldering in the ashtray. The Atlantic Ocean shimmered beyond the tinted window behind him, but he didn't look at it.

He looked at the bank memo.

Petros Global Compliance Review — Subject: Suspicious Activity Report Request.
Transaction Origin: Elmore Trading GmbH (Liechtenstein)
Amount: $3,5000,000 USD
Final Beneficiary: Mid-Town Realty Holdings – Manhattan Bridge Bank.
Meeting Requested: Patrilla, Anthony S. — w/ Compliance Officer Lara Kim & Treasury Liaison

His knuckles whitened as he held the paper tighter.

"What the fuck! We got a problem. Somebody's fucking with me."

He handed the paper to Dominic "Baldy" Vasselli, his consigliere. Vasselli stood nearby, reading the memo, swallowing hard.

"Find out who the fuck signed that wire," barked Sonny.

"Copy's got a signature," Baldy said as he deciphered each line. "Name doesn't match anyone on payroll. It looks like a contract paralegal from Belize who died two years ago. Signature's clean though—must've been lifted from old filings."

Sonny stared at him.

"Then we're looking at someone who's already had access."

Silence thickened in the room.

"This smells like an inside job," Sonny growled. "Like somebody's trying to shine a light straight up our ass."

He took a long drag on the cigar, then tapped the ashes into a crystal dish with mechanical calm.

"You ever hear of this... *Elmore Trading?*" he asked, even though he already knew the answer.

Baldy flipped through his files. In stiletto fashion, "Shell. Set up three years ago. Layered to obscure ownership. Liechtenstein registry is airtight.

Sonny's gaze hardened.

"This shit didn't come from outside," he said. "It came from someone who knew the way in. Someone who knew just what to trigger to set the whole fuck on fire."

He grabbed the receiver and stabbed the speed dial.

The line clicked.

"Yeah," came the voice on the other end. Gruff. Frankie Dellaro.

Sonny's voice was low, tight.

"I got a storm on some wires, Frankie. A bank flagged a $3.5

million transfer that runs straight through my name."

Pause.

"I want you to tear open anything in one of our companies, Elmor Trading. Who inside had access? Look into anybody who left. Anybody who got cute. Find out who's burning this shit."

He drew in another breath, slow and lethal.

"Frankie—this smells like Willoughby… or Manetti—I want them turned over before the feds find them. You got shit on your trip to New Orleans, so get back on Manetti's trail and don't get back to me until you have results. If he's alive, he'd better pray the feds get to him first."

He hung up.

Didn't say another word.

He knew where this could end.

Sonny Patrilla had just moved the family into war footing.

CHAPTER 51

THE SECRET BARGAIN

MANETTI used a burner phone he bought at a smoke shop in Atlanta to call Rossi's cell.

"Any word yet?" was his voice message.

The call came early that morning from Rossi's cell.

"It was me," Manetti said without preamble.

"You sure as hell don't make it easy, Manetti," replied Rossi at the other end.

"I needed to show them I was serious."

"And Abdullah? You really have something?" Rossi asked excitedly.

"I have bank records. The office visitor's log, internal memos. I can prove he funded the operation."

"Why didn't you tell me earlier?"

"Because it was my leverage," Manetti said. "And now it's my offer."

Rossi's instincts kicked in. "You understand what this means, right? The minute the Treasury and the Attorney General see that name connected to 9/11 financing, it's not just a federal case—it's a geopolitical earthquake."

"I know," Manetti said. "That's why I'm offering testimony. I want immunity. Full protection. Not just for me—Andrea, too."

Rossi exhaled. "I'll call Gallagher. See if we can set up a meet, asap."

******

At the U.S. Attorney's Office, the morning after the *Tribune* scoop on Abdullah's donation, phones were ringing before the doors even opened. Treasury. State. The White House. The *Tribune story* had triggered controlled chaos.

Assistant U.S. Attorney Justine Gallagher stepped into her office carrying a black coffee and found Ava Ramirez already waiting.

"You saw it?" Ava asked.

"I saw it," Gallagher replied.

"Could it be Manetti again?"

Gallagher didn't respond at first. Then, "Rossi just confirmed it. He has proof. Says Manetti's ready to testify."

Nathan Park appeared in the doorway. "We just got a ping from Treasury. They want to know what we know and how fast we can move."

"Get them off our backs," Gallagher said. "We don't know anything yet. Not officially. Not until we talk to the source."

Park nodded. "What's your play?"

"I want it quiet. Controlled. No leaks, no press. And we do it off the grid."

Ava folded her arms. "You're going to meet him?"

"I'm going to hear everything he's got. Then I'll decide if he walks."

******

Gallagher contacted the State Department to request a secure location for an off-the-record intelligence meeting. The response arrived within hours.

A historic estate outside Leesburg, Virginia, built in the late 1800s, once served as the home of a U.S. ambassador to Britain. It received high-security upgrades after 9/11. Off-grid, off-record, with no media trail. The estate was used for diplomatic asylum seekers, secret meetings of foreign officials, and unacknowledged strategic sessions.

Meeting date: January 3, 2002

******

The snow was light on the day of the meeting. The winding drive into the Blue Ridge foothills curved past quiet horse paddocks and frost-covered oak trees. The stone mansion sat on thirty acres, protected by pines, stone walls, and electronic security. No signs. No staff visible. Just two black Suburbans and three U.S. Marshals stationed at entry points.

Mike Manetti, alone, stepped out of the vehicle in silence. He wore a navy pea coat bought that morning at a kiosk in Reagan Airport, with a scarf tucked neatly under his collar. He carried a leather satchel heavy with secrets.

He was escorted through a spacious entry hall into the drawing room, where Assistant U.S. Attorney Justine Gallagher stood at a long table, flanked by DOJ Deputy Counsel Richard Taylor, a State Department liaison, and a silent man from the CIA whose name was never offered.

Gallagher didn't smile.

"You've got a lot of people's attention, Mr. Manetti," she said coolly, offering her hand and moving the session to a conference table. "And a lot of people are asking why now."

"Because the truth was rotting in my head since I learned of Abdullah's connection to Hanjour," he replied while taking a seat. "I'm not doing this for anything but my feelings of guilt, for my unknowing involvement in facilitating funds for the hijackers. I'm coming forward voluntarily with information that I think is important to national security and to help your investigations into the terror attacks."

Taylor spoke next, skeptical. "You worked for Simon & Kershaw. A firm now obliterated, records mostly destroyed. And you expect us to believe you kept the good stuff… for what reason?"

"I kept most of it as insurance—dealing with Sonny Patrilla, Abdullah, and several other clients," Manetti said. "Because I knew what I was doing could be risky for me. Dangerous because of my inside knowledge of my clients' businesses and the fear of becoming a scapegoat. Eventually, someone was going to need a thread to pull. I didn't want it to be me."

Gallagher's eyes narrowed. "You're asking for full immunity. That's a big ask—especially from someone who admits laundering money for a financier tied to the 9/11 hijackers."

"I understand what I'm asking for is big, but what I offer is bigger. The Abdullah connection is big enough to warrant my request, but I can provide documentation on others of interest to you and to other law enforcement abroad," Manetti explained.

Manetti set the satchel on the table, unzipped it, and said, "Let me show you why I deserve immunity."

He removed three encrypted flash drives, a bundle of legal folders, and two envelopes. "These contain internal ledgers from Simon & Kershaw, routing instructions, trust documents, and nominee agreements. Every shell company I helped set up. Payment trails from Zaid Abdullah to accounts used by Hani Hanjour. I moved funds for him—once—on Abdullah's instructions. I didn't know who he was then. I do now."

Gallagher didn't look away. "And we're just supposed to take your word on that? You expect this room to believe you were a patsy who just woke up with a conscience?"

"No," Manetti said. "I expect you to verify everything. I kept records—visitor sign-in sheets with Hanjour's signature, Abdullah's too. Once you trace the payments, you'll see the network. Foreign national trust accounts linked to Gulf-region shell companies. Funds funneled through art sales, offshore banks, and fake mining contracts. It's detailed information, not just about Abdullah. It's the Patrilla crime family, corrupt bankers, and European industrialists who didn't want tax exposure."

Taylor leaned over the files and opened one. His brow rose. "You're naming names."

"Yes, and I'm giving you leverage," Manetti said. "A roadmap to some of the dirtiest money on earth."

The man from the CIA finally spoke. "How do we know you're not using us to settle a score or bury someone bigger?"

Manetti didn't flinch. "I'm not settling scores. Being trapped in the South Tower on September 11th and later discovering that the attack was funded by one of our clients, I came to realize that what I had always thought of as victimless crimes do have consequences.

I've found a new path, a new life. I want to make amends by exposing some of what I've done. With the assurances I want, you'll have my full deposition under oath. I'll swear to it in front of a grand jury if need be."

Gallagher crossed her arms. "Let's hear it, all of it."

"Immunity for all activities related to Simon & Kershaw. No federal or state prosecution. Full witness protection. A sealed identity. Relocation. No public testimony. No leaks. And my sister Andrea is protected, too. No subpoenas. No surveillance. She knew nothing."

Taylor glanced at Gallagher, then back to Manetti. "And what about Christopher Willoughby? You worked with him. Laundered funds with him. You're asking for protection for him, too, aren't you?"

"I am," Manetti said quietly. "He's dead. Died on 9/11. He didn't know who he was really dealing with. They used him the same way they used me—through our greed and vulnerability. He can't defend himself anymore. I doubt he knew anything about Abdullah's plans. The sheikh was just another wealthy client with special needs that we could handle. I see no reason for his name to be linked to this tragedy. Don't let his kids grow up with his name dragged through this."

Taylor's voice was incredulous. "You want us to shield a dead man?"

"I want you to leave his name out of your indictments. Sealed or otherwise. That's one of the prices for me walking into this room."

Gallagher paced for a moment, weighing the political cost.

"If your files are real," she said, "they could put pressure on multiple fronts. Treasury, Justice, and even foreign governments. But if this breaks wrong—if your documents are incomplete, or false, or unverifiable—you're back on the table. Understood?"

"Understood," Manetti said. "But I think you'll find I've come with the goods."

Gallagher turned to her team, "Let's hear your story, and we'll begin the document review. Mr. Manetti, we'll start deposing you this afternoon. If your evidence holds up, we'll present it before a federal grand jury under seal. From there, I'll make the recommendation to the Attorney General and initiate the immunity protocol."

The CIA representative added quietly, "The moment this goes upstairs, it becomes a diplomatic issue. You know that, right?"

"I do," Manetti replied. "But this link will begin unmasking others involved and bring you closer to the truth."

******

Over the next two days, Manetti walked them through everything.

The meetings with Adbullah regarding his business transactions, the sheikh's visit to the office to meet with Willoughby, and shortly afterward, Willoughby's detailed request to Manetti to arrange the funds for Hanjour. Manetti provided the visitor log, which documented Abdullah's visits and the one-time visit by Hanjour to pick up the briefcase containing cash and cash equivalents.

Manetti outlined the process of laundering Patrilla's money. He supplied bank accounts, passwords, and wire transfer details. He also provided evidence of other clients' money laundering activities. Some names might be recognized by the public.

He didn't use notes.

He didn't flinch under pressure.

When it was over, two days later, Gallagher set down her pen, slid a file toward the State Department liaison, and finally broke her silence.

"Mr. Manetti," she said. "The material and statement you provided are impressive, and, I must say, explosive. After reviewing your affidavit and supporting material, I will recommend full acceptance of your immunity request to the Attorney General. From there, it will proceed through legal and classified diplomatic channels. The Abdullah connection is no longer just a matter of tax evasion or financial misconduct under FATCA."

She folded her hands.

"This involves intelligence, international banking, and counterterrorism. Whether any of this ever becomes public is not my decision. However, the evidence against Abdullah is actionable regarding 9/11 connections, tax fraud, art smuggling, and illegal finance. We will coordinate with foreign partners, secure warrants, and start an investigation that will make his life very difficult."

She picked up one of the flash drives and nodded to the State liaison.

"All original materials will be archived under State Department classified retention. This meeting never happened. You were never here. And as of now, your existence—Michael Manetti—ends in this room."

"What about Sonny Patrilla, and the art cases?" Manetti asked.

Gallagher hesitated. "The FBI will pursue Patrilla with the material you provided. With your leads and detailed account structures, and their investigation, we'll have enough for indictments. As for the art, the FBI, in cooperation with other national law enforcement agencies, can follow up on domestic connections and can work with Interpol on the foreign leads. But for right now?" She tapped the Abdullah folder. "This is our priority."

Manetti stood, his eyes cold and resolute. He left the meeting with verbal assurances. A car was waiting to take him to the airport and return him to Key West. He turned to Nathan Park, shook hands, and said, "Then I guess I'm done running."

CHAPTER 52

THE DECISION

THE conference room on the fifteenth floor of the St. Andrews Plaza Federal Office Building was cold, brighter than it needed to be. Fluorescent lights hummed against the pale walls, and a panoramic window framed the East River in slate gray.

Having returned to Manhattan from the Virginia estate meeting, Assistant U.S. Attorney Justine Gallagher stood at the head of the table, arms crossed, her eyes fixed on the stack of files laid out in front of her. Her team waited. Nathan Park, deputy chief for investigations, with his usual yellow legal pad already full of scribbles. Special Agent Walker from the FBI's Organized Crime Task Force. Ava Ramirez, senior analyst, her laptop open, screen already glowing with data.

Gallagher tapped the blue folder in front of her. The one that had come back from Virginia.

"This," she said, her tone flat, "is no longer theoretical. Manetti gave us enough to open every Patrilla account like a Christmas stocking. We have confirmation of shell companies, the wire transfers, and—most importantly—the cycle of money laundering he personally set in motion. The question is: do we use it now, or do we sit on it for something bigger later?"

No one spoke right away. The silence was deliberate. This wasn't a case you hurried into.

Nathan Park leaned forward, pen tapping against his legal pad. "FinCEN and Treasury are already on it from the transfer Manetti orchestrated. If we wait, we risk losing momentum and maybe a seat at the table. Sonny's already paranoid; he hasn't been moving around like he used to. If Sonny starts smelling smoke, he'll torch half these companies before we get another look."

Ava Ramirez nodded but slightly raised her hand. "True, but let's not kid ourselves. RICO is heavy, but the family has survived sweeps before. If we go now, with what we have, Sonny goes down, but will the structure remain? Can his organization withstand his loss? Would they plug someone else in? If we wait, if we peel back more layers, we can take down more than Sonny—we can clean the whole table."

Walker cleared his throat. His voice had the clipped edge of someone who had spent too long in interrogation rooms. "We're not going to dismantle the mafia in one shot. That's fantasy. Sonny's the head of the New York snake. Take him, and you rattle the rest. Let it ride longer, and we lose him. He's careful, but not immortal. He's in his sixties now. That paranoia that Park mentioned? It makes men sloppy."

Gallagher looked at Park. "Run me through what we actually have. Forget the theatrics. What's admissible, what's solid?"

Park flipped through his notes. "First, the wire Manetti staged— Concordia to Trio Verde to Elmore to Petros Global in Miami. It's neat, it's documented, and it lands directly into a Patrilla-controlled account. The cycle is textbook money laundering, that's one count, clean."

"Second, Manetti gave us access logs—signatures, internal memos, routing instructions. They line up with transactions the Bureau's already been monitoring. That's corroboration."

He paused and checked his notes again. "Third, we have historical data: the older shell companies linked to Sonny—Trio Verde Capital, Elmore Trading GmbH. We can tie those to at least three previous FBI files, dating back fifteen years. Fraud, extortion, tax avoidance. Always too circumstantial to stick. With Manetti's documentation, we connect the dots."

"And Sonny's name?" Gallagher asked.

Park slid a sheet across the table. "He's listed as the beneficiary on at least three trust accounts we know about, tied to Elmore Trading, Mid-town Realty Holdings, Inc. at Manhattan Bridge Bank, and Petros Global in Miami. And we've traced other payouts to assets in his wife's name — a townhouse in Staten Island, and a condo in Miami."

Ava Ramirez interjected. "That's the kind of nexus we've been missing. Not just cash movement, but cash into lifestyle. Homes, cars, accounts. That's RICO gold."

Gallagher nodded slowly, lips pressed thin. "And what about witnesses? We've got Manetti. Anyone else?"

Walker shook his head. "No one credible yet. Willoughby's dead, and everyone else is either too dirty or too scared to talk.... until we turn up the heat. Manetti's testimony is the backbone."

"Which makes him both our greatest asset and our greatest

liability," Ava said.

Gallagher allowed herself the faintest of smiles. "Welcome to prosecution."

She turned a page in the blue folder. It was all there—what Manetti called the Canary Ledgers, the accounts, and the faint smell of revenge in Manetti's careful notes. Enough to choke a jury. But she knew the risk: Manetti's testimony had to be secret, as they had already agreed. If they didn't use him now, he could be lost to them forever.

"Let's game this out," Gallagher said. "We move now: we convene a grand jury, we present the evidence, and Manetti's affidavit, and the property links. What happens?"

"A few dozen counts," Park said, matter-of-factly. "Racketeering, extortion, wire fraud, money laundering, tax evasion. The works. Sonny goes away for life. No parole. Leavenworth or worse."

"And if we wait?"

Ava hesitated. "We risk Sonny cleaning house. These shell companies are ghosts. He could dissolve them tomorrow, further offshore the assets, and what we have starts looking weaker. Still admissible, but a weaker trail."

Gallagher leaned against the table, her palms flat. "So the choice is certainty now, or higher ambition later."

Walker shrugged. "Ambition gets people killed. Sonny has hitters. Co-conspirators and witnesses disappear. Manetti's already afraid they're after him."

The room went quiet again. Gallagher let the silence stretch until it was taut.

Finally, she spoke. "All right. We move. We take what we have and build the case in the open. RICO charges, federal grand jury, subpoenas to every bank in Sonny's Rolodex. We go hard and fast."

Ava closed her laptop with a click. "Then we need to prep the financial story clearly. A jury won't follow every detail and distraction. They require a straightforward narrative: Sonny directed, Sonny laundered, Sonny profited. Everything else is noise."

Gallagher nodded. "You and Park build that line. Walker, I want your task force coordinating with the marshals. If Sonny even breathes the wrong way around any potential witnesses, I want him in cuffs before he knows we're watching."

She straightened, the decision made. "We're done pretending we don't have enough. We have enough. The press will scream for details. The defense will scream louder. But in the end, Sonny Patrilla will rot in a federal cell. And he won't be coming back."

Park scribbled one last note on his pad. "Grand jury first thing Monday?"

"Grand jury first thing Monday," Gallagher confirmed.

They all stood at once, the energy shifting. Files tucked under arms, chairs scraping back. It felt more like the start of a war than a meeting.

Gallagher lingered behind, looking once more at the blue folder. The transcript from Virginia. Manetti's testimony. His conditions. His cooperation.

She closed it gently, slid it into the locked cabinet on the wall.

For a moment, she stood alone, listening to the hum of the lights.

Then she whispered to herself, "One down."

******

Two months later, the U.S. Attorney's Office for the Southern District of New York announced the unsealing of a 27-count grand jury indictment charging Anthony "Sonny" Patrilla, leader of the Patrilla crime family, and several associates with racketeering, extortion, bribery, and money laundering offenses.

The charges stemmed from a coordinated investigation led by a federal-state task force with the help of the Attorneys General of New York and New Jersey.

At a federal courthouse press briefing, Assistant U.S. Attorney Justine Gallagher said, "This indictment strikes at the core of one of the most entrenched organized crime networks operating along the Eastern seaboard. For decades, the Patrilla family corrupted businesses, banks, and public institutions through fear, fraud, and financial crime. That influence ends today."

The indictment claimed criminal activity covering over twenty years, including plans to launder illegal proceeds through domestic and international banks. Gallagher confirmed that related investigations are still ongoing.

CHAPTER 53

THE MARINA AMBUSH

FRANKIE Dellaro, under direct instruction from Sonny Patrilla, had been back on Manetti's trail since the Elmore Trading transaction exposed money laundering. Embarrassed by failing to follow through on his last attempt, Dellaro kept his search quiet from Sonny. He would only tell Sonny once he had eliminated Manetti.

Dellaro returned to Key West carrying a suitcase that looked like it was borrowed and a face that belonged to a different city. He walked like a man who could map an alley with his eyes closed; head tilted to one side, shoulders relaxed, with a gaze that touched every reflection in every window. He was hunting, and the island would feel it.

He began with the places where names are traded for tips: vendors at Mallory Square, waitresses at noisy bars, a barber smoking in the doorway of a shop that hadn't seen a remodel since the '70s. He described his man—big city look, average height, fit build, mid-thirties, square shoulders, careful with his words, not a tourist.

Most shrugged. Too many drifters. Too many snowbirds. But

late on the second afternoon, a fisherman with a sunburned neck and a bucket of pinfish squinted and said, "City guy like that? I think I've seen him at Fisherman's Net a couple of times. He helps around the *Kitty Jo*—Jim Foster's boat. Quiet fella. Keeps his head down."

"Where can I find this *Kitty Jo* boat?" Dellaro asked.

Pointing in the direction of the wharves, the fisherman said, "You can find it at the charter docks, that way, a couple of blocks."

Dellaro nodded and slid a twenty into the man's hand. "Appreciate the civic spirit," he said sarcastically.

He spent the next few hours in the shade of the icehouse near the charter slips, a cigarette parked behind his ear, pretending to read last week's sports page. The charter office was a weathered clapboard rectangle on pilings, with light leaking around crooked blinds. The faded sign out front read FOSTER FISHING CHARTERS in hand-painted blue letters. Boats bumped and squeaked against their fenders. Gulls heckled from the pilings. The air was a stew of diesel, cut bait, and salt. The *Kitty Jo*'s slip was empty.

He asked a dock hand when the charters usually returned for the day. He was told "around dusk." The boats were usually in by then, and the crew would be cleaning up before heading home for the evening. Dellaro returned after dusk and waited for any activity around the office or the dock. Around 6:30 p.m., he saw three charter boats approaching through the breakwater. He watched each to see if any would be coming toward the Foster dock. The first boat continued past. The second maneuvered toward him. As the boat turned to dock, Dellaro caught the name *Kitty Jo* painted on the transom. He watched as the guests, weary and sunbaked, gathered their belongings, cheered their excursion with the remaining cold beer from the cooler, and departed with ice-filled bags of their catch. Dellaro eyed the two crew members; the older man was clearly the captain. The crew member was a husky, leathery-skinned guy in his late twenties. Dellaro had met Manetti on a few occasions and quickly knew neither was his target.

After an hour cleaning the boat and stowing gear for the next day's work, the younger man left the boat and dock. The captain stayed a bit longer before heading to the charter office, where he stayed for only 30 minutes.

Dellaro, on a gut feeling, decided to surveil the office for a while longer. He positioned himself in the shadows and waited.

Around ten p.m., Dellaro spotted a man walking on the dock and heading toward the office. The man approached the shack, unlocked the door, and entered. Dellaro waited, then moved closer. Through the window blinds, he saw him: alone at the stand-up desk, sleeves pushed to the elbow, head bent over the desk. He recognized the same man who had sometimes met with Sonny—quiet, clean, a man who kept puzzles in his head. "Manetti," Frankie said under his breath, with a bitter taste on his tongue.

******

Manetti promised Jim he would take a stab at establishing a workable budget for the business. One that would cover the newly restructured bank loan. He reviewed the accounts, the history of charter reservations, typical operating expenses, and the new loan payments; then added a cushion for unexpected repairs bound to arise.

The dock was moonlit between passing clouds, the air close with humidity. Rain was expected overnight. Water gently slapped the pilings with a slow, patient rhythm. A fluorescent lamp hummed over the bait freezer, casting a dull cone of light across the deck boards. Inside the office, a lamp glowed over the standing desk; Manetti was fully absorbed in his work and didn't hear the footsteps behind him. The door had been propped with a chock of wood to coax air through the place. A box fan shuddered in a corner.

The dock was deserted and quiet. Dellaro slipped through the door without a sound, a length of chain picked up outside the shack wrapped once around his right fist and looped at the wrist. "Evening, counselor," he said.

Manetti looked up, and for a heartbeat the room froze—the desk, the lamplight, the man with the chain. Recognition flickered across Manetti's face, which then went hard.

"Frankie," he said with surprise and fear, "What are you doing here?"

"Been looking for you since a stunt was pulled on Sonny. Your pal Sonny wants answers." Frankie smiled, "He wants to know who jammed a hot iron in his pocket. He's thinking you did something clever you shouldn't have."

"You've got the wrong guy," Manetti said. "I left all that behind."

"Cute." Frankie stepped closer. "What I got is you, down here, playing fisherman, while certain wires blow a hole in certain ledgers. Sonny gets embarrassed. He don't like being embarrassed. So he sends his best listener to find you. He's gonna love knowing where you've been hiding." He lifted the chain a few inches. "I listen with this."

Manetti said, hands open, palms out. "I don't know what you're talking about."

The chain whipped through the air as a blur. It cracked against Manetti's ribs with a sound like breaking twigs. He curled around it, a grunt tearing from his teeth, and staggered backward into a pile of anchor chains that rattled like maracas.

"Again," Frankie said, conversationally. "Names. Who else knows?"

Manetti forced the air back into his lungs. "There's nothing to tell."

Frankie pushed into him, crowding, all forearms and shoulder, and the smell of tobacco smoke. "You burned Sonny. Besides Sonny, only you and that piece of shit Willoughby had access to that account, and Willoughby's dead. So that only leaves you. Who helped you do it?

"I don't know what—"

The chain flashed again. Pain flooded brightly through Manetti's head. He hit the edge of the bait tank, and the tank hit back, sloshing a cold, foul sheet of water over his shoulders. Frankie's hand was at his collar and on his belt. Dellaro lifted Manetti by the belt, his back arched over the fiberglass tank. He saw the ceiling fan spin once, twice—a lazy pinwheel. Then Frankie shoved his head into the tank.

Saltwater, scales, and cold, dirty water. His nose burned like fire. He kicked, twisted, yanked, but Frankie had a butcher's grip, hips set wide, weight in the right places. Manetti's lungs lit up in panic. Frankie hauled him out just long enough for a gasping cough and then pushed him under again.

"Who else, counselor?" Frankie's voice was flat, close to his ear each time he came up. "Who got paid? Somebody at that Miami bank? Who's your help?"

Manetti gagged, coughed up, and blinked water out of his eyes. "I don't—"

Down again. Cold went to freezing. The world shrank to bubbles, noise and the thud of his pulse. His hands scrabbled for a lifeline and landed on the lid of the tackle box. It was heavy, slick with brine. He yanked it free, tore it loose with a yank born of terror, and swung blindly toward Frankie's head.

The edge of the lid caught Frankie across the cheekbone with a hollow crack. Frankie cursed, and his grip loosened just enough for Manetti to twist sideways and plant both feet on the wet floor. He shoved off the side of the tank like a racing swimmer, and the two of them fell into a tangle. The lid clattered across the desk and bounced to the floor.

Frankie recovered quickly, muscles coiling. He whipped the chain with a sideways arc; it missed Manetti's face by an inch and instead shattered a fluorescent tube, strobing the room into flashing light and shadow.

"Lucky," Frankie said, breathing harder now. "But you ain't slippery enough."

He came again, and again the chain caught ribs, a line of fire that stole breath. Manetti backed up, eyes scanning for an advantage, for tools...for anything. His palm slapped the wet deck; his fingers slid over a coil of line and a stainless-steel gaff with a parrot-beak hook. He closed his hand around the shaft and felt the weight of it, a fisherman's leverage.

"Frankie," he said, voice raw but steady. "You don't have to do this. He doesn't need—"

Dellaro answered with a feint left, then whip-snapped the

chain right. Manetti lifted his hand with the gaff; the hook knocked the chain off course with a clang that jolted Manetti's shoulders. He lunged forward smashing his boot into Frankie's shin. When Frankie bent instinctively, Manetti drove a second kick higher, hard and mean into the groin. Frankie's breath whooshed out in a grunt, and he dropped to one knee, one hand reaching for the desk to lever himself up again, rage blooming hot in his eyes.

Manetti took a swing of the hook.

The gaff's tip found a soft target. It stabbed low into Dellaro's throat, deep enough that his next words came out as a wet gargle. Shock flashed across his face like a short circuit. He staggered backwards, hit the tank behind him, and slumped. Blood leaked like a slow faucet down the shaft of the hook embedded in his neck.

Time thinned; the night held its breath. Then panic slammed back into Manetti, and he did the only thing his animal brain had left—he took Frankie by the hair and shoved his head into the bait tank and held it there while the chain slid off Frankie's fingers and the air in his chest bubbled to the surface… until the bubbles stopped.

It felt like years and yet no time at all. Now the water in the tank was bloodied and still. Dellaro was still.

Manetti let go of Dellaro's neck. The chain was still dangling from Dellaro's wrist. The office smelled like fish and fear.

He leaned both hands on the desk until the shaking settled enough to move. He wiped his mouth on the back of his sleeve and tasted salt and blood. He stood, swayed, shut the lights, and found the door with his shoulder and closed it tight, leaving Dellaro headfirst in the tank…dead.

******

By now it was raining. He didn't run. In pain, he walked slowly, which kept the world from tilting too much. In a few minutes, he reached the Foster home...the porch light a small beacon in the dark.

Emily opened the door on the second knock. She took one look at him and her face changed. "Oh my God. Dean—what—"

"Water," he managed. "And... I need Jim."

He told the story twice: once to Emily in the kitchen, where her hands trembled as she pressed a dish towel soaked in ice water against his ribs, her gentle touch soothing. Then again, to Jim when he came home, wet boots thudding on the wood floor. Manetti's voice was raw but steady -- because it had to be. He didn't leave anything out. He no longer had room inside him for more lies.

"Frankie Dellaro?" Jim said, almost a growl. "You're sure."

"I'm sure," Manetti answered, his voice quiet, but final.

Jim ran a hand down his weathered face, then paced once across the living room and back. "If Dellaro's here, maybe someone else is too. Do men like him work alone?"

"I doubt anyone else was with him," Manetti said. His chest tightened as he forced the words out through bruised ribs. "Sonny gave him a long leash. Dellaro bragged about it. Said Sonny didn't want to hear from him until I was finished. Dead. If he had backup, they would've come through the door with him."

Emily still hadn't let go of his hand. Her thumb traced the lines of his knuckles, slow, mechanical, like she was trying to rub life back into him. Her eyes shone glassy, but her jaw was set.

"We have to call Dusty," she said suddenly. "We can't hide a body. We can't carry this ourselves. We call him and we tell him..."

Jim wheeled on her. "Tell him what?" His voice cracked on the word.

Manetti blinked hard, looking between them. "Who's Dusty?"

Emily answered softly, but there was steel under it. "Sheriff Raymond McGraw. Dusty. He's been Dad's friend for years. He's straight and decent. If anyone can help us, it's him."

Jim stopped pacing, hands on his hips, staring at the floor. "Dusty's my friend. He's family in some ways. But that doesn't mean he'll risk his badge. He'll need more than trust. He'll need a story that makes sense when it comes out. That's his job. He's got to defend every choice he makes."

"All the more reason we tell him the truth," Emily shot back. "At least the truth we can give."

Jim shook his head, softer now. "Honey, the truth drops Dean right in the middle of it. You start talking about "mob,' 'money laundering,' and 'Patrilla'—you're putting a federal target on Dean's back. I don't know how you and Dean could live with the consequences, certainly not here in Key West. Besides, Dusty can't just sweep that under the rug. He won't."

Emily turned, eyes blazing at Manetti. "Then what? What can we live with?"

Manetti swallowed against the ache in his ribs. The pain was sharp, but the weight in the room was heavier. "I don't know," he admitted. "Dragging a sheriff into this isn't smart. The press would have a field day. It risks all of you. Even if I'm gone tomorrow, you still have to live here, face whatever fallout there is. I won't leave that kind of shadow over you."

Emily's hand tightened around his. "You're asking me to watch you be hunted in silence. That's not an option anymore."

The room fell silent, the kind of quiet that hums like a storm on the verge of breaking. Jim stared at the floorboards, as if the right answer might be embedded in the grain. Emily moved closer, her voice softer but still urgent.

"We have to do something, Dean. We can't keep reacting. If we don't reach out, if we just sit here—next time maybe it's not you who gets hurt."

Her words hung there. Jim exhaled hard through his nose, but didn't argue.

Manetti leaned back in his chair, his chest rising slowly and heavily. His mind analyzed the angles, just like he used to with ledgers and accounts. Dusty was a risk. But silence was too. Maybe there was another way.

Finally, he spoke, voice low but gaining steadiness as he said it. "Maybe Dusty isn't the only option. There's someone else who can take this higher, someone who can make it vanish."

Jim frowned. "Who?"

Manetti looked up, the decision settling in his bones. "Justine Gallagher. The U.S. Attorney I met with in Virginia. She already knows the story and the players. She has given me assurances. If there's anyone who can protect you and keep me out of a shallow grave, it's her. We give Dusty the break-in story to cover the local ground, if we have to. But the rest—the truth that matters—goes to Gallagher. Quietly. Direct."

Emily's eyes searched his face. She could see the weight of it pressing on him, but also the resolve hardening there.

"You think she'll protect you?" she asked.

Manetti didn't answer, then said, "I don't know why I didn't think of this sooner. My head has been a mess all night. But, although it's not official yet, I've been granted protection under my agreement with the government for situations like this," he said. "Now is the time to activate it."

The three of them sat there, torn between fear and trust, between lies and survival. The storm outside had passed, but inside that house, the air felt charged—like lightning still searching for a place to strike.

Manetti picked up the phone and dialed.

******

Manetti dialed the number with trembling hands; the number Gallagher gave him in Virginia—a lifeline tucked away for nights exactly like this. The old-style ringtone was answered instantly.

"Code?" the voice demanded.

"D.B. Cooper," Manetti said, barely above a whisper.

There was a pause as the officer cross-checked the registry, unaware of the significance of the name Manetti adopted as his U.S. Marshal code name. "Authorization number?" the officer asked.

"34135."

The line went silent for a beat. Then: "Stand by. I'm connecting you now."

At 12:35 a.m., the red emergency phone in Justine Gallagher's Manhattan apartment buzzed to life. She rubbed the sleep from her eyes, turned on the lamp, and picked up the phone from her bedside table.

"Yes. Talk.", she said sleepily.

"Miss Gallagher, it's Mike Manetti. I've got trouble." His voice was fatigued but firm. He told her everything—the attack, the fight, Dellaro's dead body, how Emily and Jim had patched him up, and how he couldn't involve the sheriff without exposing them all."

Gallagher listened, asked pointed questions, then cut him off. "Stay put. Don't involve anyone else, especially the sheriff. Don't let anyone in that office, understood? We'll handle it. You'll be met at the address you gave me," she hesitated as she looked at her watch, then continued "give them a few hours...should be before sunrise."

Manetti breathed once, hard. "I understand, thank you."

"We'll be in touch when this is over," Gallagher replied, then abruptly disconnected.

******

By 1:15 a.m., two black Suburbans pulled from the underground garage beneath the Federal Building in Miami. Engines low, tinted windows, plates federal government issue. They merged onto I-95, headlights on, in military precision, the two vehicles slicing south through humid blacktop until the interstate narrowed to U.S. Route 1, then the long, thin ribbon of the Overseas Highway. Bridges arched like bones over ink-dark water. The drivers said little. Radios muted.

At 4:02 a.m., the Suburbans rolled onto Stock Island, then into Key West proper, ghosting down Roosevelt Boulevard. They cut their lights two blocks from the marina.

Manetti stood alone in the parking lot, jacket pulled tight, ribs screaming with every breath. The smell of salt and diesel clung to everything.

Two Marshals approached: one tall with cropped hair; the other built thick, his voice flat.

"You 'Cooper'?"

"Yes."

"Where's the body?"

Manetti led them inside the office. The fluorescent light buzzed overhead, casting its sickly halo across the scene. Blood streaked the floor, bait water pooled dark around the tank. The gaff hook was still lodged in Dellaro's throat.

The lead marshal crouched, studied the body with the detachment of a man who'd done this a hundred times. He noted the chain, the overturned tackle box, the scuffs that told the story of the fight. He lingered over the tank for a moment, then stood.

"ID?"

"Frankie Dellaro," Manetti said. His voice was steady now. "Sonny Patrilla's man. Prints will prove it."

The marshal didn't argue. "Phone? Wallet? Keys?"

"Don't know. Didn't look."

Behind them, the second Suburban's doors opened, and four figures in white Tyvek suits emerged, carrying black Pelican cases. They moved like a pit crew—quickly, silently, and precisely. Within minutes, they had body-bagged Dellaro, mopped, bleached, and reset every chair and rod holder in the area. The chain and hook were cleaned and stowed away. By 4:45, the air smelled only faintly of disinfectants and the sea. To anyone entering at sunrise, the office would appear untouched

Manetti stood outside as the vans pulled away, taillights gone before dawn broke.

******

In a small Key West cottage, Emily Foster sat at the kitchen table waiting for Manetti to return. Jim Foster lingered in the doorway looking out across the docks - silent, but present, a sentinel in work boots.

Sonny Patrilla waited for a phone call from a man who would never make a call again. The trail to Manetti died with Frankie Dellaro at the bottom of a federal incinerator bin.

Manetti still had one last act. He handed over files and names related to stolen art to Rossi for the FBI's Art Crimes Unit. Raids swept across Europe. Museums rehung works once thought lost.

Emily's world expanded—she continued her work with R.E.E.F. and founded a marine rescue nonprofit that rescued injured sea birds and helped stranded whales and turtles return to the sea. She raised funds and recruited allies to expand their reach.

For Manetti, the past would never be erased, but he no longer measured his worth by money moved in shadows. He lived quietly under his new identity in Key West. He had recovered stolen treasures, taken down mobsters and financiers, and bought himself redemption. The charter business he rebuilt with Jim Foster thrived. He earned his captain's license. Eventually, Jim handed the company over to him and Emily.

As dawn spilled pale gold light over the docks that morning, he looked toward the horizon and saw his future with Emily. He inhaled a deep breath of hope and finally felt a breeze of peace.

CHAPTER 54

EPILOGUE

THE memorandum was stamped T**OP SECRET / National Security.** A blue folder, sealed and numbered, was hand-delivered to the National Archives. Inside: the full transcript of a secret January meeting at a State Department estate in Virginia's horse country.

He gave the U.S. government what it needed—evidence that Zaid Abdullah, a Saudi businessman tied to the Royal Court, bankrolled a financial network that funded the 9/11 hijackers. Then, unlike the man whose code name he used—D.B. Cooper—he started a new life, but with immunity and witness protection.

The White House officials read the document in silence. Prosecution was impossible; diplomacy required discretion. Instead, backchannel deals were made. Abdullah's empire was broken up, his influence limited. At home, he faced charges of tax crimes and asset concealment—quiet punishments aimed at ending his reach without causing scandal. The message from Washington was clear: never consider funding attacks on the United States or its foreign interests again.

Abdullah's empire crumbled. Counterterrorism units mapped his financial trails, exposing European cells, shutting down their operations, and preventing attacks. Two years later, while under investigation by Italian authorities, Abdullah was killed in Riyadh when a truck bomb tore through his convoy. His strategist and driver died with him.

Emil Dubois faced questions from Bahamian banking regulators, waved forms and signatures that proved "compliance," and discreetly paid off the proper official. Two months later, he was gone—retired and relocated with his family to the Tyrolian Alps of Italy.

Andrea Manetti voluntarily left her job in Manhattan to relocate to Wilmington, North Carolina, where she continued her career as paralegal.

Rocco Rossi received quiet commendations from the FBI and a plaque from the insurance industry honoring his role in recovering stolen art. He returned to Trenton, a few pounds heavier, a bit wiser, and definitely prouder.

The New York Tribune – **Newsroom , March 2002**

The room had thinned out, along with the late-afternoon sunlight. Copy editor Melissa Ford hunched over her desk, running numbers on a scratch pad for a follow-up article on the Adbullah donation. She froze mid-calculation.

"If you split Abdullah's $744 million across the official count of 2,977 victims," she said aloud, tapping her pencil, "you get $249,916.02 each. Odd number, don't you think? Why not round it up?"

She punched the figures again, this time subtracting one name.

"Huh, 2976 victims… that's exactly $250,000 each."

She swiveled toward Martin Karsh's desk. "Why would the math work only if there's one fewer victim than the government count? Could it be just a clerical error?"

Karsh leaned back in his chair, the glow of his monitor reflecting off his glasses. He didn't answer right away, letting the silence press. The clatter of the keyboards of a nearby reporter's desk only sharpened the pause.

Melissa frowned as she read off her notes. "The passenger and crew lists match for all four flights. Pentagon casualties accounted for by their tight access controls. Police and fire rosters add up. Which leaves only the civilian count at the Trade Center. Two thousand, two hundred and three. But the donation number suggests exactly one fewer."

Karsh's voice was low, almost to himself. "One victim short… or one survivor sending a signal."

Melissa's eyes narrowed. "You really think—?"

APPENDIX: PRESS COVERAGE

Boston Beacon

May 31, 2002

Two Gardner Masterworks Recovered in Plea Deal

BOSTON – Twelve years after the infamous Isabella Stewart Gardner Museum heist, two stolen masterpieces are finally on their way home.

Manhattan prosecutors announced Thursday that Gianni Giulietta, a convicted New York mobster, agreed to return the works in exchange for avoiding a death sentence on multiple murder convictions. Earlier this month, a jury found Giulietta guilty in the slayings of four Long Island rivals whose bodies were discovered in a Catskills quarry. Judge Leopold Kravitz is expected to ratify the plea next week, remanding Giulietta to life in state prison.

Assistant District Attorney Carolyn Kunisch told reporters the deal was struck in cooperation with the FBI and the U.S. Attorney's Office for the Southern District of New York. *"These priceless pieces will be restored to the Gardner Museum, where their empty frames have waited for more than a decade,"* Kunisch said. *"Mr. Giulietta will never walk free again."*

In a written confession, Giulietta admitted he acquired the art shortly after the 1990 theft, knowing it was stolen. For years, the paintings were hidden in a closet at his New Jersey shore house before being moved to the Delaware Freeport warehouse as potential collateral for future deals.

Investigators say Giulietta's statement has already provided new leads into the original heist and the art's shadowy movements in the years since. "Sometimes justice takes an unusual turn," Kunisch added. "Without this cooperation, the masterpieces might have remained lost for generations."

The recovered works, still unnamed publicly, will undergo authentication before their formal return to the Gardner. Eleven stolen pieces remain missing.

******

Athens Dispatch

March 26, 2002

Al Qaeda Linked to Stolen Greek Antiquities Recovered from German Tech Mogul

At a joint news conference in Athens today, Greek officials, representatives of INTERPOL, and the FBI announced the recovery of more than 100 looted antiquities tied to what investigators describe as an international smuggling network with suspected links to Al Qaeda.

Among the recovered artifacts were miniature sculptures dating to the mid-sixth century B.C., including an eight-inch stone figure of a young man valued at more than $15 million. Officials confirmed that the pieces were seized from properties owned by German technology billionaire Karl Steiger, who was taken into custody in Luxembourg earlier this month.

Authorities said Greek artifacts were found at Steiger's estate in Luxembourg City, aboard a Mediterranean yacht, and inside storage crates at Geneva's Freeport warehouse, a facility long under scrutiny for shielding illicit art transactions. In all, 110 items were recovered, with an estimated market value exceeding $100 million.

The raids followed an anonymous tip delivered to INTERPOL and the FBI, leading to a multi-agency operation involving Luxembourg police, Swiss national authorities, and INTERPOL's art-crime task force.

"These artifacts are not only treasures of Greece, but they are also treasures of humanity," Andreas Papandreou, Chief Curator at the National Antiquities and Art Museum, said in a written statement. "Their return ensures they will inspire future generations, not serve as shadow assets for criminal networks."

Investigators disclosed that digital records recovered from suspected Al Qaeda operatives in Germany detailed the movement of stolen antiquities through European freeports, bolstering suspicions that the artifacts were being used to launder money and finance terrorist operations, including the September 11 attacks.

While Steiger faces charges of theft and unlawful export of cultural property, law enforcement sources suggested that indictments could extend far beyond a single billionaire. "This case has already touched high-profile individuals—government officials, businessmen, even celebrities," one European investigator said, speaking on condition of anonymity. "And more arrests are coming."

The case has cast new light on the global antiquities trade, a shadow market estimated in the billions, where stolen artifacts often vanish into storage, used as collateral in secret financial dealings.

******

Roma della Sera
April 29, 2002

Villa on Lake Como Raided
Saudi tycoon's estate tied to stolen art investigation

COMO – The Lake Como residence of Saudi businessman Zaid Abdullah, already in the spotlight for his high-profile donation to the 9/11 Victims' Fund earlier this year, became the target yesterday of a Carabinieri raid.

The Cultural Heritage Protection Squad seized ten major artworks long missing from European museums. Two paintings were found displayed in the villa itself, one in a bedroom, another in an office, while the remaining pieces were discovered still crated in a Livorno freeport facility, likely untouched since their theft.

"Roughly eighty percent of stolen art ends up in vaults or freeports, hidden from law enforcement and tax authorities," one investigator explained.

Authorities estimate the works span three decades of theft across the continent. Specialists called to the scene suggest that some pieces may include "blood art"—paintings and sculptures stolen by the Nazis from Jewish families in Germany and France during World War II.

The raid, part of a months-long undercover probe, followed a string of anonymous tips and was carried out in coordination with international law enforcement.

Though Abdullah has not yet been charged, police sources indicate further inquiry will determine his role in the storage and concealment of the art discovered in Livorno. Experts in looted wartime collections have already been asked to assist in the identification process.

******

Le Courrier de la Seine
13 September 2002

International Bank at the Heart of Money Laundering Affair

BRUSSELS – Belgian authorities confirmed yesterday the indictment of two senior executives of the European Commerce Bank N.A., accused of orchestrating an international money laundering network that operated for more than twenty years.

The men, Hans Edlemann, a Swiss national, and Julius Kraus, of Germany, were arrested Tuesday during a daylight raid at the Geneva Freeport. Investigators seized a cache of stolen art allegedly destined for transfer to a Russian national.

Among the recovered works were a Van Gogh and a Monet, taken in Sweden fifteen years ago from a private collection, as well as a Kandinsky that vanished during transit at Heathrow Airport in 1996 while on loan from the National Museum of Norway. At the time of the theft, authorities described the Kandinsky as a significant loss in the history of modern art; its recovery marks a rare victory against international traffickers.

The identity of the Russian intermediary arrested during the operation has not yet been disclosed.

Officials noted that the raid was the culmination of a long-running investigation into the European Commerce Bank's practices. Anonymous sources close to the case suggested that the operation's timing may have been precipitated by intelligence from an undercover agent.

This latest scandal highlights the role of freeport facilities in facilitating the circulation of illicit wealth, often hidden behind layers of secrecy. For investigators, the arrests mark a decisive step in exposing the financial infrastructures that have allowed criminal organizations to operate across borders with near impunity

AUTHOR'S NOTE AND DISCLAIMER

As of this book's publication in 2025, none of the thirteen masterworks stolen from the Isabella Stewart Gardner Museum in 1990 have been recovered. Any depictions of their discovery or return in this novel are entirely imagined. The museum's $10 million reward for information leading to the safe return of the missing artworks remains active and publicly offered.

Escape From Ground Zero is a work of fiction. Names, characters, businesses, organizations, places, events, and incidents are either the product of the author's imagination or used in a fictitious manner. Any resemblance to actual persons, living or dead, is purely coincidental.

ABOUT THE AUTHOR

Michael Zoglio is a retired entrepreneur, business consultant, and volunteer mentor to small businesses. For twenty years, he was a licensed private investigator specializing in locating missing persons. He previously authored the classic *Tracing Missing Persons: A Professional's Guide to Techniques and Resources.*

www.ingramcontent.com/pod-product-compliance
Lightning Source LLC
Chambersburg PA
CBHW020910130726
47904CB00006BA/1811